"Who is it that hurt you so deeply?"

Adam's question came like a bolt out of the blue.

"What are you talking about?" Jane whispered.

"Your defenses are up against men in general. And it's because someone hurt you in the past."

"You're wrong! There wasn't anyone! Why don't you just leave me alone?"

Jane got to her feet, but Adam was beside her in a flash, his hand firm on her shoulder. "You can't run away from me, Jane."

She looked up at him uncertainly, trembling beneath his touch.

Adam sighed. "Ah, Jane. You're an incredibly beautiful girl. One day a man will come into your life who'll love you so much he won't be deterred by all your barriers. And he won't take no for an answer...."

Never Say Never

Claudia Jameson

Harlequin Books

TORONTO • NEW YORK • LONDON
AMSTERDAM • PARIS • SYDNEY • HAMBURG
STOCKHOLM • ATHENS • TOKYO • MILAN

Original hardcover edition published in 1983
by Mills & Boon Limited

ISBN 0-373-02578-5

Harlequin Romance first edition October 1983

CHAPTER ONE

'I LOOK forward to meeting you on Monday, then.' Jane Winters spoke clearly and concisely, if not altogether truthfully, to the voice on the other end of the line.

'You can skip the pleasantries,' the voice barked. 'Just make sure you have all the information with you. I want to see copies of all the correspondence, understand?'

'Yes, Mr Francis.' She gave the telephone receiver a disparaging look, not that it did any good. Adam Francis was totally unaware of her irritation, which was just as well, since he was the company's most important client. It certainly wouldn't do to offend the owner of Francisco Enterprises!

'And have you made a note of my other requirements?'

'Yes, Mr Francis.'

'Right. I'll see you at eight on Monday.' He'd hung up before Jane had a chance to say anything else.

She looked thoughtfully at the telephone receiver. Had Adam Francis been particularly curt today or was it just Jane's mood which was making her less tolerant, her worry over her father? She pondered over this for a moment before carrying on with her work. No, there'd been nothing out of place in her attitude towards Mr Francis; she never let her worries, or any aspect of her personal life, interfere with her work. The rudeness had been entirely on Mr Francis' part. He was always businesslike and curt at the best of times, but he'd been particularly offensive today. Probably because his latest plans had been thwarted, she thought. He wasn't used to things going wrong.

In the year that Jane had been with this company she had had plenty of dealings with Adam Francis. She had written and sent telexes to him frequently to every corner of the globe, and had spoken to him on the telephone quite often when her boss, John Brinkman, was unavailable.

Brinkman, Clayton & Brinkman, Solicitors at Law, had offices in several countries. The London branch was the biggest and they had at least one specialist for every aspect of the law. John Brinkman's speciality was property matters—and Adam Francis was a property developer, an old-established client who gave the company a great deal of business. On Monday Jane would actually get to meet the man. He was coming to London for a few days and, because Jane's boss would then be away on a well-earned holiday, she had to meet Mr Francis at the airport.

She was by no means looking forward to meeting him, but she did admit to being curious about him. There were people who worked hard and there were people known as workaholics, but it seemed to Jane that Adam Francis was in a category all his own. He was absolutely dynamic. She had the impression that he spent all his waking hours working, working, working. Everything he did was successful—everything he touched turned into money. Jane's boss called him the man with the Midas touch.

She switched on her typewriter, eager to finish the draft report her boss had given her. When she heard a sudden, ominous whirring noise coming from the machine, she realised with a sinking heart that the carriage-return belt had snapped. She had heard that noise before.

It just wasn't her day. Everything seemed to be going wrong today. At least, everything seemed to be some sort of test. She had woken up to find her father in the living-room, already on his second cup of coffee and looking ghastly. His illness didn't usually show itself so plainly, and Jane had felt sick with anxiety. Of course her father had reassured her, as he always did, that he was fine—just fine. The truth was that Gerald Winters was a sick man and he would never be 'fine' for the rest of his life. True, the days when Gerald actually looked ill were rare, but they were happening more frequently as the years passed.

Gerald Winters had shooed his daughter out of the flat at her usual time, but she had been late arriving at the office in any case—thanks to a signal failure on the Underground. To top it all her heel had broken as she'd gone dashing up the escalator; her boss had gone off to an emergency meeting, leaving her to cope with the difficult Mr Francis, and now this! Not having the use of her typewriter for several hours would throw her whole schedule out, and there was so much still to be done.

Calmly, Jane reached for the telephone, keeping her fingers crossed that she could get a typewriter mechanic reasonably quickly and at the same time wondering if there was a spare machine around that she could use in the meantime. Fortunately she was not easily ruffled; if she couldn't borrow a typewriter then she'd simply catch up with the filing. Provided the objectionable Adam Francis didn't ring again, with luck the rest of the day should go pretty smoothly!

Within an hour Jane had everything under control. The filing was done and the draft report had been completed on a typewriter borrowed from the stores. She was entering her lunchtime post while nibbling her way through a cheese sandwich when one of the junior partners came in.

'Morning, Jane. Or should I say good afternoon? Working through your lunch again? John Brinkman's a lucky old dog having you for his P.A. But at least he appreciates the fact.' Paul Meekins hovered in the doorway to Jane's office, his greeting giving no hint of the way he always felt when seeing her. For the hundredth time he was struck by the loveliness of this tall, slender girl with the flawless skin and immaculate grooming. As ever, her long dark hair was coiled into a neat bun at the nape of her neck. As ever, the smile she gave him was polite but distant.

He was still attracted by her. Still intrigued by her, despite having discovered her secret. He knew, now, about Jane's private life—her love life, at least. It irritated him and it saddened him, but it didn't detract from his admiration of her. He'd never said a word to her about seeing her with her boy-friend—if that was the right word—even though Jane knew Paul had seen them together. It was, after all, her business. Jane Winters was a very private person; nobody in the company knew anything about her private life. Except him. And he would never gossip about the little he knew; he respected Jane's wish for privacy.

'Good afternoon, Paul.' Jane's hazel eyes swept over him coolly, uninterestedly, as he approached. 'To what do I owe the honour of this visit?'

'Well,' he leaned casually against the filing cabinet, smiling down at her, 'you know I'll visit you on the slightest pretext, with the smallest excuse . . .' Jane did not grant him a second smile. She was not amused. Paul Meekins was a nice-looking, ambitious young man who had been with the company since leaving university. He had only recently been made a junior partner and was very much John Brinkman's blue-eyed boy. And deservedly so, Jane thought. He was pleasant enough, but by force of habit she kept him well and truly at arm's length.

Paul had asked her out five times during her first few weeks at Brinkman's, persisting even when she had told him, truthfully, that she just wasn't interested. In an effort to put him off once and for all, she had eventually explained to him that there was already a man in her life, one with whom she was very deeply involved. That had cured him, finally. Especially when fate had lent a little assistance a short time after this revelation and Paul had actually seen her with her mystery man. The memory of that evening made Jane smile inwardly, not with amusement but with satisfaction. Paul's attitude towards her had changed since that evening. Oh, he still flattered her—but he did not flirt. And he certainly never asked her out these days.

'Get to the point, would you, Paul? I'm extremely busy.'

Paul sighed inwardly. At times she was so frosty with him that he wondered why he continued to like her so much. Why didn't he just accept that even flattery was wasted on Jane? He'd never got anywhere with her, and as long as there was this other man in her life, that would continue to be the case. He nodded his dark head towards the adjoining door of Mr Brinkman's office and waved a sheaf of papers at her. 'I need ten minutes with the boss.'

Jane's delicately-shaped eyebrows rose slightly. 'No chance. He's out at a meeting.' She held out her hand for the papers, casting an efficient eye over their contents. 'Hmm. Do you want to discuss these with Mr Brinkman or just have him check them?'

'I just want him to check them before I send them out—before he leaves for his holidays, of course.'

'Of course. Leave them with me. I'll see what I can do. We'll be going over the Francisco Enterprises stuff as soon as he gets back, but he'll probably have time in the morning. Will that be okay?'

'Jane you're an angel!'

'Paul, flattery will get you nowhere.' She matched his wry smile with a distant one of her own. As long as they understood one another, as long as Paul kept his distance, she could cope with him well enough.

After Paul had left her office, Jane smiled properly. Little did he know that there was actually no man in her life! She'd been forced to invent the existence of a boy-friend in order to stop Paul from pestering her. He wasn't to know that the man he had seen her with was only her ex-boss, David Boyd, that what he had witnessed was part of a perfectly innocent chance meeting!

Jane had bumped into David Boyd on a cold, rainy evening as she was dashing for the Underground. She had joined him for a spur-of-the-moment drink in a wine bar not far from the office—and Paul had been in there! Paul had seen them leaving together too, with David putting a protective arm around Jane as he steered her through the rain and into his car, in order to give her a lift home.

She'd never forget the look on Paul's face! Her ex-boss was in his mid-forties, but he was very smart and fairly attractive, and Paul had obviously assumed he was the boy-friend Jane had spoken of. She'd never put Paul straight on this because it suited her purposes—he had never asked her out since!

In truth, Gerald Winters was the only man in Jane's life. And that was exactly how she wanted things to remain. Her father needed her, her father was the centre of her private world. And in her public world there was her job, the work she enjoyed so much. What else did she need? In a word—nothing. She didn't need men; she wanted no complications in her life, no emotional involvements . . . no more *hurt*. In her twenty-three years she had given her heart once, just once, only to have it handed back to her, shattered into little pieces. It was something she had vowed never to do again.

John Brinkman got back to the office in the middle

of the afternoon. He walked into Jane's room with his usual calm air, the air of a man who had all the time in the world. She looked up at him and smiled. She liked her boss enormously. He was actually in his early sixties, and although he was looking a little tired of late, he certainly didn't look his age.

'Everything all right, Jane?' Mr Brinkman put down his briefcase and leaned his weight against her desk as he waited to hear what had happened in his absence.

'Everything's under control.'

'Jane, you're a godsend, you know that?' he smiled. 'You always say the same thing—everything's under control! I think if I returned to the office one day and found the building had been struck by lightning, you'd still be sitting there, telling me everything's under control!'

She grinned at him, pleased to be appreciated. As personal assistant to one of the most brilliant lawyers in London, she needed to keep on top of things, and she did so very efficiently despite her tender years. She picked up her notebook and read off a list of messages, most of which she had dealt with herself. 'The last call this morning was from Adam Francis. He was ringing from New York and told me he'd be arriving Monday evening at Heathrow at eight o'clock. I assured him I'd be there punctually, with all the papers to hand.'

Mr Brinkman frowned, suddenly looking very much in need of the holiday he was about to take. 'Good. We'll go over all his stuff before we go home tonight, then I'll spend my last day tomorrow catching up with correspondence.'

He was still frowning as he walked away from her and headed towards his own, adjoining office. Then he paused and turned. 'Don't let him hassle you, Jane.'

'I beg your pardon?'

'Adam Francis. You haven't had the pleasure yet, have you?'

'No. I'll bet it's a dubious pleasure.'

'No.' There was no hesitation. 'Adam's an old friend as well as a client, and a good man, basically. But he can be—er—very forceful at times.'

'I'll cope, Mr Brinkman,' said Jane, with a confidence she felt. Forceful he might be, but she was confident of all the facts she had to pass on to Adam Francis, since she'd double-checked all the research personally. Besides, she had always coped very satisfactorily with him over the phone, even if he was extremely curt and irritating at times.

'He'll be very put out about the Birmingham project,' Mr Brinkman went on, 'but you just remember that his bark's worse than his bite.'

Jane shrugged. 'There's little we can do for him except offer an alternative site. Besides, he must have at least a dozen other projects he can be getting on with.'

'Oh, he has, he has. But that's not the point, you see. He wants to build a hotel in Birmingham, and nothing will stop him. It'll become a matter of principle to him. He won't be thwarted by high-minded petty officials.' His laughter was almost reluctant. 'Those will be his words, Jane. You'll see.' And then he laughed properly, his eyes lit with amusement and . . . and something Jane could only interpret as respect.

'It amuses you, doesn't it, the way Mr Francis carries on his empire-building, often in the face of adversity?'

John Brinkman thought about that for a moment. 'Amuses isn't quite the right word. Admire would be better. I like a man who knows his mind, gets what he wants. He'll find a way round the Birmingham problem, just you mark my words!' He sobered suddenly. 'What about hotel accommodation—did he ask you to book something? And what about a hired car——'

'It's all reserved,' Jane assured him. 'Hotel suite, hire-car and a particular chauffeur he wanted, a Mr Johnstone.'

She saw her boss's face relax somewhat. 'Well done, Jane. If there's anything else Adam wants you to do for him, please give him top priority. Nothing will be too much trouble—remember that.'

On any other evening, Jane would have been thinking of the day's events while she travelled home. But not tonight. She wasn't thinking about Adam Francis' problems, Mr Brinkman's warning, or the fact that the typewriter mechanic didn't turn up as promised. It had been a madly busy day, and all she wanted to do now was to take a hot shower, change, relax—and see for herself that her father was all right.

She pulled her jacket closely around her, shivering as she stepped off the train and into the cold autumn wind. She had a car, an old Mini which had been her eighteenth birthday present from her father. It had been spanking new then. But she never used it for commuting because it wasn't worth the hassle and expense of trying to park in the city. In fact the only reason she kept it was for giving her father an occasional run out at weekends, when he was well enough.

'Daddy? I'm home!'

'So I hear!' Gerald's voice reached her from the lounge as she hung up her jacket in the hall.

As she walked into the room, she tried very hard not to let anything show on her face, but a sickening fear stabbed at her as she saw that her father was using his wheelchair today. It had been several weeks since he'd last resorted to that.

Gerald Winters was suffering from a degenerative disease which was slowly weakening his bones. Apart from twice-monthly injections which went a small way in slowing down the process, nothing could be done for him. The prognosis was hopeless, and eventually he would end up permanently in a wheelchair. Gerald fought against that day with everything he had in him—but it was a losing battle.

'Now, Jane, take that look off your face. I'm only using this contraption today to conserve my energy. I've got work to do tomorrow!'

Jane stooped to kiss him, her experienced eyes moving swiftly over his face. This was her way of gauging how her father was really feeling, regardless of what he told her.

'When do you see Doctor Leonard for your next injection?'

'Monday morning.'

'Daddy, let me come with you this time, *please*.'

Gerald waved a dismissive arm. 'Since when do I need you to hold my hand? I'm perfectly capable of getting to the doctor's and back.'

She didn't argue with him. There was no point. Never yet had he allowed her to visit the doctor or the hospital with him and although she worried about it, she knew she must respect his need for independence. Gerald had been a very active man in his years working as an electrical engineer, and Jane understood how much he resented his enforced inertia. As long as he was able to get out occasionally on his own, she had to let him do it.

'You need a haircut,' she smiled. Gerald's hair was steely grey, almost bald on top. He was, in fact, only sixty years old, a couple of years younger than her boss, but he looked years older. Jane turned away from him then, swallowing hard against the lump that was rising in her throat, her love for her father bringing tears to her eyes—tears he would very much disapprove of. Gerald was a demonstrative, loving father, but he would not tolerate emotional displays over his illness. 'I'll start dinner. What do you fancy?'

'Dinner's in the oven. It's lamb casserole, it'll be ready by the time you've showered.'

'But——' Jane checked herself and headed for her bedroom. That was another thing: like any other human being, Gerald had a need to be needed. He insisted on cooking their dinner on week-nights. It was, she realised, his way of making a contribution to the household, of doing something for his daughter, and while Jane would have been perfectly content to do everything, again she had to bear in mind her father's pride and his needs.

Gerald had a small pension, smaller than it would have been had he been able to stay in his job until retirement age. Occasionally he earned extra money writing articles on engineering for trade magazines. That, plus the very good money Jane earned, provided more than enough for their needs, so Jane saved every spare penny. In her case, she was saving for the rainy day she knew would arrive, the day when she would have to give up her job in order to care for her father, and it helped enormously that the flat was paid for.

When Jane's mother had died, they had decided to stay on in the house they then lived in, but two years later, when Jane was twenty and Gerald's illness had been diagnosed, they moved into the flat. 'For practical purposes', Gerald had said. It was a purpose-built flat in a reasonably smart block, and of course there was no garden to bother about. More importantly, there was a really good neighbour right next door whom Gerald could call on should he need to during the day.

In her bedroom Jane slipped into a robe, brushed down the suit she had worn to the office and put it in the wardrobe with her several other business suits. The new shoes she had been obliged to buy in a hurry that morning were put into the kitchen, ready to be cleaned later on.

She showered, as she did on arriving home every evening, washing away the dust of the city and easing away the tensions of the day under the piping hot water as it beat down upon her slender body.

Jane's life was very much a routine. At the weekends she did the shopping and ironing, and cleaned the flat. During weekdays she was constantly under pressure at the office, but in the evening she relaxed. Evenings with her father were very pleasant. Now and then, if Gerald was well enough, they would go to the cinema; occasionally they had visitors, and other evenings they would play cards or watch the television or just natter. Gerald took an interest in Jane's work and from time to time she would bring him up to date on what was happening in the office.

For a young woman of twenty-three, Jane's life would be described as dull. But she didn't see it that way. She liked her routine and didn't mind at all that she lived from one task to the next, having very little fun. There was a certain security, a certain safety in living to a strict routine. She was perfectly content with her lifestyle . . . but Gerald was not.

About a year earlier he had started urging her to go out and have some fun, 'Like any normal girl'. She had told him then that she was content, that she didn't need 'fun', that she was happy with the way she lived. Gerald had been difficult to convince, and she had convinced him only temporarily, because a few months later he had talked to her again. That time, Gerald had been very serious about what he wanted to say, and although Jane put up a good fight, she had ended up realising that she would have to do something in order to placate her father—or rather, that she would have to *appear* to do something.

It had happened just after last Christmas. Jane had been working for Brinkman, Clayton & Brinkman for about four months. During the Christmas holidays her new, high-pressure job had caught up with her and she had spent a good deal of her time falling asleep on the settee during the day.

'You're working too hard,' Gerald had said worriedly. 'Are you still enjoying your new job?'

'Very much,' Jane assured him. 'In fact, I love it! Look, Daddy, I'm sorry I've been such lousy company over the holidays. I've been going through a sort of adjustment these past weeks, I suppose, what with the longer commuting time and the extra work. I can honestly say I do about twice as much for Mr Brinkman than I ever did for David Boyd. Mr Brinkman's very efficient.'

'So are you!' Gerald smiled. He was proud of his daughter; she was quite young to be in the position she'd landed at Brinkman's. 'I know how conscientious you are. You're sure it isn't too much for you, though? I mean, the extra money isn't all that important, you know——'

'I'm certain. In fact, I'm offended you even suggest it! Job satisfaction, Daddy. You know what I mean. I get a lot of satisfaction from doing my job well. Lolling around during Christmas has just been my way of winding down, that's all.'

Jane meant every word she said. Gerald knew it, too. Still, he looked at her dubiously, and in that way she had of gauging her father and reading when something was on his mind, Jane realised that the conversation so far had just been a preliminary to something else. 'Okay, Pop, what is it that's really bugging you?'

Gerald Winters suppressed his smile at her question, at the way she'd read him. She was a chip off the old block, because he could read her, too. And he was in no doubt at all that the reasons she gave for living like a nun during her leisure time were all false. Quite false. Even if she'd managed to fool herself, she hadn't fooled him.

He didn't smile. He didn't smile because it was important to him that he got through to her this time. 'It's about the conversation we had a couple of months ago.'

Jane stiffened slightly. 'Oh. That——'

'Your life, Jane. It's all work and no play. You never have any fun. Ever since Billy, you've lived like——'

'Can't we leave Billy out of this?' Jane's voice came out far more sharply than she'd intended then. 'I'm sorry, it's just that——'

'Ever since Billy,' Gerald persisted, 'you've lived like a nun. It's unheard-of! You never go out, and for a girl of your age, it's abnormal.'

'Abnormal? Abnormal!' The word offended her, but she forced herself to laugh. 'Oh, really, Daddy! I've told you before, I'm quite happy with the way I am. I've got you, haven't I?'

'I won't be around for ever, Jane.'

It was a simple statement of truth. For Jane, it was terrifying, and she bit hard on her lip.

'Jane love, I can't tell you how much it upsets me that you're letting Billy ruin your life.'

The words, the tone of her father's voice brought Jane's head up with a snap. She had to deny that one—and fast. She couldn't *bear* her father being upset. 'Is that what you think? That Billy's ruining my life? Well, you're wrong! Believe me, Billy can't hurt me any more. You're absolutely wrong about that, Daddy.'

'Then how come you've never been out with anyone since Billy?'

Jane's heart sank. She was losing this argument because she was limited as to what she could say. How could she tell her father that nothing and nobody would come between herself and him? That she had devoted herself to him and wanted to be with him as much as she possibly could in the time he had left— however long that was? In the ensuing years he would need her more and more, and she had vowed to look after him to the exclusion of everything else, and when the time came, it would exclude her job, too.

Gerald Winters had a fear of becoming a burden. Obviously she couldn't tell him these things. He'd probably throw her out rather than feel he was inhibiting her life. He wasn't inhibiting her in any way, of course. But if for one moment he got the idea into his head, she'd have great difficulty in convincing him to the contrary.

'Jane, I said how come you've never been out with anyone since Billy?'

Then, as Jane cast about frantically for a suitable answer, came the very thing she feared. Gerald looked at her levelly, searchingly. 'If you're telling me the truth, if you're not still hurting over Billy, then it must be me. Do you stay home so much for my sake? I hope that isn't the case, Jane...' his voice grew tight and his forehead creased with worry. '... because I will not allow you to put me before yourself.'

Jane had had to be very careful how she answered him. If she had protested too much, he would have seen right through her, and that would have made him deeply unhappy.

'Not at all,' she said airily. 'You've got me all wrong. I know you can cope perfectly well alone in the evenings, and if you want company there's always Mrs Graham next door.'

'Exactly. So how come you don't accept some of these dates you're offered? Why aren't you getting on with your life?'

'What dates?' She grinned impishly, but she was

actually playing for time and something approaching fear was making her stomach contract.

'Oh, come off it!' Gerald looked at her in mock disgust. 'You're just as beautiful as your mother was at your age. And when I met her, I had to queue up to get a date with her! It must be the same for you. There are eight big companies in that enormous building you work in, apart from Brinkman's, and hundreds of men! Darling, you can't tell me that nobody's asked you out!'

If Jane hadn't been so disturbed by the conversation, she might have laughed. Gerald Winters was no fool. She had, of course, been offered dates. Paul Meekins wasn't the only one, either; she had been asked out by men outside of Brinkman's. She had managed easily to discourage them with her blunt and truthful statement of being uninterested. The discouragement of the persistent Paul had taken a little more effort—namely the invention of a non-existent boy-friend.

'Well, there hasn't been anyone who really interests me, to tell you the truth,' Jane said slowly, 'I—I'm very choosy, you know.' She was still playing for time. Her father had backed her into a corner and she couldn't see her way out of it. His urging her to go out occasionally had become a very real problem. This was the second serious conversation on the subject and it wouldn't be the last either, knowing Gerald. Unless she could come up with a solution.

'Now that I can believe!' Gerald smiled because he was making headway, at last. 'And I think you have a right to be choosy. Besides, you've changed quite a lot lately. You're more mature, so you will be harder to please. But give mankind a chance, Jane! Accept a date occasionally, at least. I don't expect miracles. Much as I would love to see you really settled—no, don't look at me like that—much as I'd love to see you settled, I realise it'd take someone really special to get a ring on your finger. But you can at least have a little fun and relaxation now and then, eh? And get on with your life.'

It was not unreasonable. For Jane, it was absolutely undesirable. But Gerald was a father, with a father's point of view, a father's natural concern. She smiled at him, loving him, and suddenly realised that the answer to this problem was very simple. Very simple indeed. 'Okay, Pop, I'll see what I can do.'

. . . I'll see what I can do. Now, as Jane towelled herself dry after her shower, she thought back over the months since that conversation had taken place. Not for the first time, she mentally patted herself on the shoulder at the way she had solved the problem. What Gerald wanted for her and what she wanted for herself were very different—and she'd found a way of keeping them both happy.

The answer had lain in Paul Meekins. It had occurred to Jane that she had solved the problem of Paul by inventing a boy-friend. Why not do the same thing with her father? And why not use Paul as her non-existent date? It was all so logical; Paul worked at Brinkman's, she knew him, so she would be able to answer questions about him.

And that was exactly what she had done. Occasionally, or so Gerald thought, Jane went out with Paul. For two reasons, she didn't date him often. Firstly she had to find something to do with herself on those evenings, and sitting alone in a restaurant and cinema was not very satisfactory. She did it, though. Secondly she kept her dates down to a minimum so Gerald wouldn't think she was getting too involved. If that happened, he would start asking to meet Paul . . . and that would never do.

It had been six weeks since her last supposed date, and it was about time she had another. Gerald had recently been asking what had happened to Paul these days . . .

Sitting before her dressing table mirror, Jane took a long, hard look at herself. She didn't exactly like what she was doing, because it amounted to deception. But any twinges of conscience were easily appeased by the knowledge that her motive was good. Her motive was her love for her father and a wish to keep him as happy as possible. And there was nothing wrong with that.

She pulled on a pair of denims and a chunky sweater, her face now free of make-up so she actually looked younger than her years. She quickly brushed her long hair, very dark brown and shining with health. At home she wore it down, held in place with a slide, but during the day she wore it in a tightly-coiled bun at the nape because she thought it more efficient like that and it didn't get in her way while she was working. Besides, she fancied that it suited her image. At work she was always immaculate, efficient, fully in control. Her public world and her private world were two entirely different spheres, kept separate, and in reality Jane would never dream of going out with someone from the office. With a wry smile she finished that thought before joining her father in the lounge: let's face it, in reality she would never dream of going out with *any* man.

'Ah, there you are!' Her father smiled, never ceasing to be amazed at the contrast between Jane, the personal assistant to John Brinkman and Jane, his denim-clad daughter who emerged from the bathroom half an hour after getting home from the office. 'You know, I read in a magazine somewhere that Gemini people are two personalities rolled into one. It's certainly true of you. You leave this flat every morning looking as if you've just stepped off the front cover of *Vogue*, but when you settle down for the evening, you look as if you'd be more at home working on a farm!'

'Thanks very much,' said Jane, with mock sarcasm. She went over to the drinks trolley and poured out two glasses of sherry. 'You mentioned work earlier, Pop. Something come up?'

'Oh, yes.' Gerald took a glass from her and positioned himself near the fireplace. 'I had a phone call from Jim Matheson today, he wants me to do an article for the December issue—basic stuff, about three thousand words.'

'Well, that's good news.'

'Have you any news? You look a bit tired, actually, did you have a hard day? Mr Brinkman's going away tomorrow night, isn't he?'

'Yes.' Jane flopped tiredly on to the sofa. 'Just for a week, but we've still had the usual panic stations, and tomorrow will be worse. Oh, by the way, since Mr Brinkman's going away, I have to meet the owner of Francisco Enterprises on Monday evening. He's arriving at Heathrow at eight.'

'Mr Francis.' Gerald nodded. He'd heard about Brinkman's biggest client. 'Bet you're not looking forward to that.'

'Not a bit.' Jane looked heavenward. 'He's a stroppy old devil at the best of times, but he's going to be hopping mad about his Birmingham project. Still,' she brightened somewhat, 'I'm having dinner with Paul on Tuesday, so that'll sort of make up for Monday night's strain.'

She saw her father's face light up with pleasure and it confirmed yet again that what she was doing was very worthwhile.

'I'm glad to hear it!' Gerald beamed. 'I'd been wondering what had happened with him lately.'

'Well, you know—he's been busy at work, just as I have. Shall we eat, Daddy? I'm absolutely starving!'

CHAPTER TWO

'THIS is Miss Winters from Brinkman, Clayton & Brinkman. I'm just checking on the arrangements for the car hire. Can you confirm that the driver and car will be at these offices at seven this evening?'

'Yes,' she was assured by a crisp and polite voice on the other end of the line, 'Rolls-Royce and driver—Mr Johnstone—will collect you at seven o'clock. Everything is arranged. We understand that you're unsure how long the car will be needed for but we'll invoice you later at the daily rate we agreed.'

'Thank you.' Jane put down the telephone and continued typing. So far, so good. Adam Francis' hotel suite was booked for four nights, regardless of the fact that he might not stay that long in London, and he had a chauffeured Rolls at his beck and call for the duration of his stay. His instructions to Jane had been carried out to the last detail.

Before leaving for the airport she would re-check the contents of her briefcase, just to make certain everything was present and correct. She was by no means looking forward to spending half of her evening with this ruthless client whose plans had been thwarted, but at least she and Mr Brinkman had come up with an alternative site for the hotel he wanted to build. That ought to placate him. All in all, she was feeling quietly confident. She'd done the best she could for their client, and she'd done it well.

At six o'clock, Jane switched off her typewriter for the day. There was an hour to kill before the car would come to collect her, so she went along to the ladies' room and put on fresh make-up. She was wearing a light grey flannel suit—just the right thing for the autumn weather—with shoes and handbag in a matching shade. Under the jacket of the suit she wore a simple, pale-blue blouse with a roll-neck. Jane did not consider it indulgent that she bought only the best quality clothes and accessories for office wear. As personal assistant to John Brinkman she had to look the part. The image reflected in the full-length mirror was very satisfactory indeed, with not a hair out of place, and she nodded to herself, her confidence increasing by the minute. She went back to her office and dialled her home number.

'Daddy? Did I tell you I'd be late home this evening?'

'Yes.' Gerald laughed. 'You didn't forget, you're far too efficient for that! You're really phoning to find out how I'm feeling today. Well, the answer is that I'm fine, just fine. I'm working on the draft of my article.'

'Good!' She knew he'd hear the smile in her voice; there was no use trying to kid him, so she got straight to the point. 'And what did Doctor Leonard have to say this morning?'

'The usual. I'm doing very well, all things considered.'

'Super. I'll see you later, then.'

'Good luck!'

At seven o'clock Jane picked up her briefcase and bag, and five minutes later she was seated comfortably in the back of the Rolls-Royce, heading for the airport. On arrival she checked that there were no delays on the flight from New York and stood patiently by the barrier beside the uniformed chauffeur. 'You've worked for Mr Francis before, haven't you?'

The middle-aged driver smiled at her. 'Yes, miss. I'll have no trouble recognising him, if that's what you're thinking about. Ah, there he is now.'

Johnstone briskly walked forward as Jane scanned the trail of first-class passengers who were just emerging from the customs area. What she saw next kept her rooted to the spot, her lips parted in an unspoken exclamation of surprise, even shock. Surely Johnstone had made some sort of mistake?

Adam Francis was nothing whatever like the man she had expected to meet. During the year or so she had been with Brinkman's, from various conversations she had had with the client, Jane had gradually drawn up a mental picture of the man.

She couldn't have been more wrong.

Not only was he years younger than she had expected—he appeared to be somewhere in his mid-thirties—but he was extremely attractive in a rugged sort of way. Handsome would not be the right word for him. Not quite. There was too much about him that was rugged, hard—even animal. No, the looks of the man who was approaching her were not handsome, but they were exciting, interesting, and for one silly moment Jane found herself wondering why John Brinkman had never mentioned how very attractive Adam Francis was ... until it occurred to her that her boss obviously wouldn't find him so!

He was a big man, tall and broad, and there was something about him that commanded attention, a strength that was more than physical coupled with an air of total self-assurance. His hair, which was a little too long, was thick and straight and brushed back carelessly from his face. It had premature bits of grey mingling with the rest of it, which was the colour of antique gold.

Not only had Jane expected a much older man, she had expected a man who would be dressed immaculately in a business suit, someone whose eyes would be stern and unsmiling. And there she was, looking at a man who seemed more like an arty film director than a property magnate. He was dressed casually almost to the point of—well, almost to the point of dishevelment—in an expensive sort of way. He was wearing an off-white safari suit and a black shirt, both of which served to accentuate the depth of his tan. The shirt was open at the neck and Jane could see he was wearing some sort of medallion, quite small, made from silver. It suited him. She didn't normally approve of men wearing that sort of jewellery—or hair that was too long—but on Adam Francis, a man who was so ruggedly masculine, it looked good.

There was something decidedly foreign about him. He lived in New York, but to the best of Jane's knowledge he was English. She concluded that it must be the depth of his tan that gave him a foreign look.

She saw him glance in her direction as he got closer. He looked away again briefly as Johnstone said something to him, then his eyes came to rest on her face. And this time, they stayed there.

Jane looked up at him. She was smiling politely, but apart from that her face was impassive, showing nothing of the shock she had experienced, was still experiencing . . . 'Good evening, Mr Francis. I'm Jane Winters. I'm pleased to meet you. Did you have a good flight?'

His eyes were intense, the most positive shade of green, and as they held hers the shock became physical as well as mental so that a tremor ran through her body. She had the peculiar feeling she was meeting someone . . . not exactly someone she knew . . . but someone she had known she would meet, one day. It was very difficult to understand. It was as if her mind were playing tricks on her and she had perhaps dreamt about this man, or someone had once described him to her in detail. Yet she knew that was not so. In those few moments she had the distinct feeling she was recognising someone she had never set eyes on before. It was illogical and very disturbing.

Automatically she had proffered her hand. It was enveloped briefly in his warm, strong clasp, and the tremor that shot through her body this time was like an electric shock, so that she wanted to pull her hand away before the formal greeting, brief though it was, had been completed. Jane silently thanked heaven she was not given to blushing, because a warmth suffused her body—caused, no doubt, by her confusion, this feeling of recognition. For one silly moment she thought Adam Francis had experienced a similar feeling, because his brows drew together in a frown as his eyes continued to look deeply into hers.

Then the reason for his frown was made plain. 'So you're the voice on the other end of the telephone,' he said quietly. 'Well, well . . . John never mentioned . . .'

The voice, at least, was not a surprise to her. Its familiarity, the deep resonance of it with its mid-Atlantic accent, or lack of accent, instantly dispelled her confusion. Jane mentally told herself off for her stupid reaction on meeting him. All right, looking now at this attractive, casually dressed man with his easy manner and slow smile, it was difficult to associate him with any of her preconceived ideas. His appearance had been a total surprise to her. But that was all there was to it.

She kept her polite smile on a face that remained otherwise impassive. 'You were saying—Mr Brinkman never mentioned what?'

They started walking towards the car park, and it was a moment before he answered her. 'Let's just say I was expecting someone older. John's never had such a young assistant before.'

It was a blunt remark, and Jane had no idea whether he was pleased, disappointed—or what. But as he looked down at her she saw that his eyes were dancing with laughter. She was instantly irked. So he thought it was amusing, did he? Well, if Adam Francis associated youth with inefficiency, he'd soon find out he was wrong!

She squared her shoulders a little, taking care to keep her irritation out of her voice. 'Mr Brinkman sends his regards, by the way. He said he's sorry to miss you. You know he's on holiday for a week.'

'I'm very glad he is,' came the easy reply. Then, astonishing her completely, he added, 'I'd much rather spend the evening in your company.'

Jane wasn't sure how to answer that, if she should answer at all. She was momentarily nonplussed. It hadn't always been easy, but she had never had any trouble handling this man over the telephone. She had known what to expect then—and it certainly wasn't charm! *Was* this an attempt at charm, or was it that he was not prepared to take her seriously, because of her age? Everything about him was so unexpected that her confidence started to dwindle.

They walked in silence for a while, with Johnstone carrying the luggage a few paces ahead of them. Adam Francis covered his ground quickly, his strides long and positive, those of a man who knew where he was going—in every sense. Yet he moved with the easy grace of a jungle animal, and Jane caught herself watching him from the periphery of her vision. She was a tall girl, and today she was wearing medium heels, but Adam Francis dwarfed her, making her feel almost petite and suddenly aware of her own femininity.

Irrationally she felt a flash of resentment towards him for making her feel like that, for the overall effect he was having on her. Mr Francis' attractiveness was an undeniable fact, but it was of no interest whatever to her. She would not let it affect her.

The best thing would be to get straight down to business, she decided. The one thing she was certain of was that Mr Francis was wholly business-orientated. Once they started talking business she would be on perfectly safe ground.

'It's a pity about the Birmingham site, Mr Francis, but we've come up with a very feasible alternative. It's a few miles west of the site you originally wanted but Mr Brinkman thinks——'

'Not now, Jane.' He cut her off in mid-speech, but he did it very nicely, smiling an incredibly attractive smile which revealed strong white teeth. 'We'll have dinner first, then we'll talk shop.'

Jane stopped in her tracks. Dinner? It simply hadn't occurred to her that she would be required to have dinner with him. She had envisaged spending an hour or so going over the contents of her briefcase, taking her client's instructions and then leaving him to his own devices for the rest of the evening. She had planned to be home with her father by eleven or so.

'What's the matter?' Mr Francis turned to look at her, frowning.

'Oh, nothing!' They'd almost reached the car, and Johnstone was holding the door open. Jane slipped gracefully inside, feeling a sudden nervousness crawl inside her stomach as Adam Francis got in beside her. She caught the faint whiff of his after-shave, something with a very earthy scent. 'Didn't you have dinner on the plane?'

He looked vaguely annoyed. 'I don't eat plastic food. What is it, Jane? Are you in a hurry to dash off somewhere?'

'Not at all.' She smiled at him warmly, wishing she had never opened her mouth. She had annoyed him, and that was the last thing she wanted to do. This was Brinkman's most important client and he expected to be treated as such. It was just that the idea of sharing a meal with him didn't appeal to her in the least. She had made up her mind about this client before she'd even met him, which was a stupid thing to do. Now she didn't know what to make of him.

'I thought perhaps you had a date later on?'

'No, no ...' Jane shook her head, the smile still fixed on her lips.

He glanced down at her left hand. 'You're not married or engaged, so it must be your boy-friend who's given you the night off?'

'Tonight was reserved for business, Mr Francis,' she said as pleasantly as she could.

There was that slow smile again, and one eyebrow raised questioningly. 'Is that all? Now that I've met the voice at the other end of the telephone, I was hoping we could make it a pleasurable evening, too.'

There was something quite ambiguous about his smile then and Jane didn't know what he was insinuating—if anything. All she knew was that her nervousness increased and so did her annoyance. This man wasn't taking her seriously, she was sure of that now. She was willing to have dinner with him, because Mr Brinkman would no doubt have done so had he been here, but that was no reason for him to be so casual, even familiar! The object of this meeting was business, not pleasure, and Jane wanted to be treated by Mr Francis with the same respect—and distance—with which he would have treated John Brinkman.

'I'd imagined you to be the sort of man who never mixes business with pleasure.'

'Really? What gave you that idea?'

'Just an impression.' She had put it mildly, very mildly. What she really meant was that she had fancied him to be a workaholic, thinking about nothing other than money. She was proved wrong again.

'I never make hard and fast rules. If I find myself in a situation where I can mix business with pleasure, like tonight, I make the most of it. I take it you accept my invitation.'

'Of course.' She had no choice but to accept, and Adam Francis knew that as well as she did. But his innuendo had not gone unnoticed, and for that reason she thought it best to qualify her answer. 'I realise you and Mr Brinkman are old friends, as well as business associates, but I'll try to ensure that your evening with me will be as successful as the evening you'd have had with him, had he been available.' She gave him one of her distant smiles, like the ones normally reserved for Paul Meekins. That should cure him of his irritating attempts to charm her.

It didn't. Her carefully worded answer, her aloofness, served only to amuse him. To her intense annoyance, Adam Francis threw back his head and laughed. 'My dear girl, if John were here instead of you, no doubt we'd have spent the entire evening talking shop. And that isn't necessarily my idea of a successful evening. But he isn't here. You are. And very pleased I am about it, too. Personally I'd like to relax for a while, have a leisurely dinner, get to know you, and then spend a little time on business. Now, how does that sound to you?'

It sounded positively frightening to Jane. She didn't want him to 'get to know' her. Nor did she want to spend a couple of hours 'relaxing' in his company before she could get away. She wanted to get very explicit, she wanted to tell Adam Francis that she *never* mixed business with pleasure. But she was in a very awkward position. She couldn't give this client the cold-shoulder she was so practised at giving. Nor could she be rude to him in any way. Besides, she hadn't yet weighed him up properly. Was he interested in her as a woman, or was he just amusing himself because she was female and young, and not at all the person he had expected to meet?

In a voice that didn't sound at all convincing, she replied, 'It sounds lovely.' Nothing will be too much trouble—remember that. Her boss's words were echoing round her head, helping her to keep her tongue in check but doing nothing for the nervousness and acute irritation that was growing inside her.

Seemingly satisfied, Adam Francis settled back comfortably in his seat, his intense green eyes appraising her openly. Jane shifted awkwardly, unconsciously edging farther away from him.

'So what do you normally do with yourself during the evening, Jane?'

'Oh, not a lot,' she said lightly, pleasantly. 'You know how it is, there's always something to be done at home.'

'Really?' His eyes mocked her. Again they were dancing with laughter. She still couldn't weigh him up. What on earth was going through his mind now? For some obscure reason she felt a blush rising in her cheeks, which, for her, was most unusual. She wasn't normally the blushing type.

'Where do you live?' he asked.

'West London.'

'Alone?'

'No.'

'Oh?'

She didn't like the inflection, the curiosity. He was doing this deliberately, trying to get a rise out of her. Wasn't he? Whatever—she wasn't about to volunteer anything. If he wanted more detail he'd have to ask.

He asked. 'With whom do you live then?'

'With my father.'

'And your mother?'

'No.'

There was a sudden silence, and Jane looked away from him. He seemed vaguely annoyed again. As before, he didn't say anything, it was just a feeling that was communicated to her. But he'd obviously got the message that she didn't want to talk about her personal life, because he changed his line of questioning.

'How long have you worked for John?'

'Just over a year.'

'Where did you work before you worked for John?'

'Another solicitors.'

'Smaller than Brinkman's?'

'Much.'

Adam Francis shifted round in his seat, crossing one powerful leg over another as he moved. His eyes were serious now, glinting in the lights from the passing traffic and looking incredibly green, incredibly beautiful. 'Tell me, Jane, are you always this standoffish—or are you just shy? Somehow, I don't get the impression that you're shy . . .'

Jane apologised at once. She hadn't wanted to indulge in a conversation about her personal life, but she didn't mind talking about her career. She hadn't intended to seem standoffish. She sighed inwardly. This man put her on the defensive; she felt threatened by him. If she were honest, she was not as immune to him as she wanted to be. There was something— something so *physical* about him. His nearness in the car was disconcerting, very disconcerting. And she still wasn't sure how to handle him. In view of his earlier comments she didn't want to encourage him, yet she certainly didn't want to offend him. Consequently she was becoming stilted and was making a complete mess of things.

Luckily for Jane, Adam Francis was not easily offended. He was astonishingly easy-going. 'Apology accepted,' he said. 'But tell me something—when you met me at the airport, you looked at me as if you knew me. Do I remind you of someone you don't like?'

Oh, but he was perceptive! So he'd read her face, when she'd thought she was giving nothing away. Little did he know how chaotic her thoughts had been at that moment. 'No. Not at all.'

'Then why don't you relax a little? Try calling me

Adam, for a start. Just relax, Jane, and forget that I'm a client.'

'Well, I can hardly forget that,' she smiled.

'You can if you try.' He was watching her closely. 'Anyway, I might be a client, but I'm not an ogre. Don't you enjoy a little flirting now and then?'

'Oh!' said Jane, genuinely taken aback. 'So that *is* what you're doing!'

It was the look on her face! He threw back his head and laughed, deep, rumbling laughter that might have been infectious in any other circumstances. 'Certainly!'

Things didn't improve, however. Jane simply couldn't reconcile the idea of having a flirtation with the company's most important client. With anyone, for that matter. She found Adam Francis audacious, to say the least. The hell with it, she thought at length, I'm not required to like him, as long as I'm polite to him.

The traffic was heavy and by the time the Rolls pulled up at the entrance to the hotel in Park Lane it was already nine o'clock. Despite the luxury of the car, Jane had been tense and uncomfortable during the journey. Chatting to Adam Francis had been excruciatingly difficult. He didn't want to talk shop yet, and that left her with very little to say to the man. He had asked her more questions, personal questions, and she had answered them as briefly as possible. She didn't want to talk about herself and her home life. Besides, he was only asking idle questions, and she resented it, thinking him rather nosey.

They had resorted to an inane conversation about various airlines, their staff and the services they had to offer. Mr Francis had been bored by that conversation, and hadn't attempted to hide the fact. All this served to make Jane feel more and more awkward and she was acutely aware that she was on duty, obliged to entertain this client until such time as he saw fit to talk business.

As he had been by Johnstone, Adam Francis was

recognised and greeted before he even got through the main entrance to the hotel. The doorman greeted him by name, as did the receptionist and the young porter who took them up to the suite of rooms. Johnstone was dismissed for the evening, told to leave the car in the hotel car park and to call for his client at eight in the morning.

Jane was a little bewildered by all this. She wondered why, when she had never before reserved accommodation in London for him, Mr Francis was so well known by the hotel staff. Clearly he had made visits to London which had nothing to do with Brinkman, Clayton & Brinkman.

As they entered the hotel lift, Jane asked him about it. 'You've been in London recently, Mr Francis?'

'No,' he said pleasantly, 'why?'

'It's just that everyone seems to know you.'

'I tip well,' he said. And that was the end of that conversation. It was as if he were giving her a taste of her own medicine and volunteering nothing.

As the lift doors opened, the young porter turned and grinned at her. It was probably the result of what he'd just heard. Nonetheless, Jane became suddenly selfconscious about entering hotel rooms with Adam Francis late in the evening. It was something that would never have occurred to her had he been the crotchety, older, businessman she had expected. But her surroundings temporarily distracted her from the thought.

The suite was gorgeous! Talk about luxury. Jane put down her briefcase and took a seat in the corner of the sitting room, where the carpets were ankle-deep, the decor Wedgwood blue and white. The period furniture and the atmosphere was much more like that to be found in a comfortable home rather than a hotel. But this was no ordinary hotel, and this was no ordinary room. It was the best suite of rooms in the finest hotel London had to offer. And Adam Francis took it all for granted.

'If you'll excuse me, I'd like to take a shower before we have dinner.' The deep voice broke into her thoughts and she looked up to find Mr Francis standing in the doorway, one of his suitcases in his hand.

'Oh! Well, y-yes, of course, Mr Francis.'

'Are you going to call me "Mr Francis" all evening? I've told you, call me Adam, okay?' He turned on his heel and vanished.

Jane, growing more selfconscious by the minute, hardly heard him. She was telling herself it was only reasonable that he would want to shower after his long journey.

Just as she'd thought this, he called to her from the next room. 'Help yourself to a drink, Jane. Believe it or not, that ornate piece of furniture at your side is actually a drinks cabinet. You'll find a good selection in there.'

Jane got to her feet and pulled down the front section of the cabinet. Sure enough, there was a compact, well-stocked miniature bar housed there, which had everything in it from lemonade to whisky. It didn't occur to her to drink anything alcoholic—she felt she needed all her wits about her to get through the rest of this evening.

She was sipping at a glass of still orange when Adam Francis reappeared—wearing nothing more than a bath towel! Jane's mouth fell open and she looked away quickly. Trying very hard not to show her disapproval and her anger, she started fiddling with the contents of her handbag.

Adam strode over to the drinks cabinet and poured himself a large Scotch. 'Hasn't the ice been delivered?'

'I—what?' Jane hardly knew where to look. Had any other stranger done this to her she'd have told him outright to go and put some clothes on. *What ever did he think he was doing?*

'The ice, I rang down for . . .' His voice trailed off and suddenly he was laughing. She knew at once that his laughter was aimed at her. Again. She was furious.

'My girl, you're so English!' he roared. 'You're all embarrassed because I'm not dressed. Look at you! Why on earth don't you relax?'

'I'm perfectly relaxed!' she said tightly. There was a knock at the door and she shot to her feet. 'I'll go!'

'That's okay, Jane, I'll——'

'Please!' She overtook him rapidly. 'Please allow me. You don't want to answer the door looking—looking like that.'

Adam Francis didn't stop her. He turned away quickly because he was having trouble stifling his laughter.

When she came back with the ice, he was sitting in the chair opposite hers. 'Would you mind?' He waved his glass at her and she went over to him and held out the bucket. He didn't move.

Jane was very conscious of his state of undress. There wasn't an ounce of excess weight on this man; he was just big. His magnificent chest was covered with a mass of fair, curly hair, and the very sight of it disturbed her. Oh, but he'd gone too far! He'd done this deliberately. She saw it as an act of disrespect, as if he were mocking her.

He still made no move to get his own ice. Jane glared at him and carelessly plonked two pieces of ice into his drink. So! There was a battle of wits going on now! For some reason he seemed set now to embarrass her or to put her down in some way. She had no idea why this should be so, except perhaps that he was still annoyed with her for being so-called standoffish in the car. But they weren't on a date, for heaven's sake! They were two strangers having a business meeting, and Jane wished he would behave accordingly.

He was taking advantage of her. He knew she was at

his beck and call while her boss was away, and he wasn't taking her seriously. He hadn't taken her seriously from the moment he'd set eyes on her at the airport. Flirting, indeed! Did he think she'd been sent along merely to amuse him for the evening?

She thought of her boss's warning not to allow herself to be hassled by Mr Francis. What did Mr Brinkman know about him that Jane did not? There was only one possible answer to that: Adam Francis must disapprove of women in business. Young women, at any rate. She thought again of his opening remark at the airport. It had in fact occurred to her that this important client might resent having to deal with the boss's assistant, but she hadn't expected to be made fun of because of her age or her sex! She wished Mr Brinkman had warned her more explicitly.

Struggling for control, she promised herself that before this evening was out she would make sure Adam Francis took her seriously. She backed away from him and sat down again, now fully composed—or so she thought. 'Mr Brinkman sends his regards, by the way. He said he's sorry to miss you while you're in town, but he——'

'You've already said that, but never mind.' He shrugged. 'I'll be over again soon. Besides, I'd rather look at your face over the dinner table. You're far prettier than he is.'

'What time does the restaurant close?' She ignored his remark, fighting frantically against her anger. She felt as if she were about to explode.

'I thought we'd have dinner in here.'

'*In here?*' Without thinking about it, she'd shot to her feet. If he were anyone other than a client, she'd really give him a piece of her mind!

'Why not?' he said lazily. 'If we eat in the restaurant, I'll have to put on a tie!' He said it as if it were something to be dreaded.

It was as much as Jane could take. She turned on him viciously. If she were going to get anywhere with him, she'd have to clear up one or two things. Right now! 'Mr Francis, are you trying to send me up, for some reason?'

He looked genuinely surprised. 'Why should I want to do that?'

'I really don't know!' She could hear the fury in her own voice.

'Would you care to be a little more explicit?' He saw her hesitation. 'For heaven's sake, Jane, go on! Speak your mind. Forget who I am. You've already made it perfectly plain to me that you're here only as a matter of duty. *Did* you have to break a date to be with me tonight?'

'No, of course not! I've told you——'

'Then you must have taken an instant dislike to me at the airport.'

'No!' He was putting her totally in the wrong now, and that wasn't fair. He was being very clever about it, too.

'Then why are you so uptight?'

'I'm not!' Her voice had risen. 'It's just that I—I didn't expect things to be like this. I mean, I— you——'

Very calmly, very quietly, he said, 'I wish you'd explain yourself, Jane.'

'You bet I'll darn well explain myself!' Jane's head came up proudly and she moved around the room like an animal that was trapped. 'I get the distinct impression that you disapprove of me because I'm a woman. Firstly, you said you'd expected someone older. Then you put off talking business until after dinner. You admit to flirting with me in the car. We come here to your rooms, and you say flattering things to me. You join me for a pre-dinner drink wearing nothing more than a bath towel, and then you tell me you want to have dinner in your rooms! What am I supposed to think, Mr Francis? I can't tell—I just can't tell—whether you're out to seduce me or whether you're trying to make a fool of me!'

There was no holding her now. In those few moments she didn't give a care what she said. 'I was sent here tonight to do a job and you seem to be making it hard for me deliberately. If you don't want to deal with me because I'm young, or because I happen to be female, then you'll have to wait until Mr Brinkman gets back. Or deal with someone else in the office. But please stop treating me as if I were nothing more than a sex object to be flirted with and teased. Yes, I am on duty, and I'm finding it very unpleasant. And yes, I am inhibited because you're a client—and don't you just let me know it!'

There was a terrible silence.

Jane slumped into her chair, and her heart plummeted. What *had* she done? In trying to assert herself, and her position, she'd really overstepped the mark! Adam Francis' face had changed completely. His eyes were as cold as green ice, narrowed speculatively. There was a muscle working in his jaw, and his lips, normally sensuously full, had tightened into a thin line. And the silence just went endlessly on . . .

Dear heaven! She should have tried harder to contain her anger instead of giving vent to it! This man was as hard as nails, she knew that. If he complained about her to Mr Brinkman, her job would be in jeopardy.

His eyes were still locked on to her face, and though it was what she wanted more than anything, Jane couldn't look away from his scrutiny. She thought him like a computer assimilating a stack of data before it spat out its answer and she stiffened, afraid of what he'd say to her.

Then, suddenly, he smiled. Fully, warmly and sincerely he smiled as if he were thoroughly satisfied with whatever had gone through his mind. His eyes travelled slowly over Jane from the top of her head to the tip of her shoes and he nodded approvingly.

'Well done, Jane! How very nice it was to get a reaction from you. A *real* reaction!' He swallowed the last of his Scotch, and Jane watched him like one who was mesmerised. 'But let me put you straight on one or two things . . . I don't disapprove of women, young or old, out of business or in business. I like women! And I like women with a certain amount of business acumen. I am not, as you put it, trying to make a fool of you—I have no reason at all to do that. You work for John Brinkman, and that's good enough for me. It means you know your job. John sent you here tonight when he could easily have sent another partner; that's a good enough reference of your capabilities, so there's no need for you to get paranoid.

'Neither am I out to seduce you, you're not my type. Have you got that, Jane? You're not my type. Oh, you're a beautiful young woman—much as you try to hide the fact. And *that's* something I don't like about you—you try to hide your femininity. I like a woman who's all woman, and revels in it. And that has nothing to do with equality, before you get on your high horse. I regard men and women as equal. But they're *different*. And I believe in enjoying that difference. That's why I said this evening would be different from the one I'd have spent with John; that's all I meant. There were no hidden meanings lurking behind my remark. But if you resent a little harmless flirtation or charm—well, that's your hang-up! And boy, are you full of them! Don't look at me like that, I'm telling you. You're inhibited and riddled with hang-ups, and it has nothing to do with my being a client. Your defences are up against men in general. No doubt you have your reasons for that, but that's your business. I shan't ask you about it, you've made it perfectly clear you don't want to talk about yourself . . .'

He got up and crossed over to the drinks cabinet, poured himself another Scotch and sat down again. And he never stopped talking for a moment. His voice was not raised, but there was a very hard edge to it and Jane, stunned into disbelief, could feel the colour draining from her face.

'. . . You know, where I come from, people work hard and they play hard. They enjoy themselves. They taste life, they feel emotions, they laugh spontaneously, they enjoy the simple things of life. They don't section life off into little compartments—you can do this now, this then, and this only in certain circumstances. Do you follow me? They don't make life black and white. If you do that, you miss all the shades in between.

'You need to open up, Jane. You shouldn't be afraid of letting one part of life overlap on to another. Take life as it comes, and enjoy it. That's my way. I get what I want from life, certainly, but I take each day as it comes. I live as I choose to live. I told you I wanted to relax for a while. I'd spent eight hours on a plane, and I needed to relax for a while. And you read all sorts of ulterior motives into that! I tell you, if I'd been with John Brinkman, the Archbishop of Canterbury or the Prime Minister it would have made no difference to me—I'd still have come in here wearing a towel. It happens to be a habit of mine, okay? I am as I am. It just happens to be my bad luck that I'm spending the evening with the stuffiest, most proper, staid and inhibited—and very English—female I've encountered in all my life!'

And that was it.

They glared at each other until Jane was forced to avert her eyes. Her face had gone from white to pink and never in her life had she known such embarrassment. He'd been hard on her; hard, cruel and unsparing. But worst of all, there was so much truth in what he'd said.

Something inside her seemed to collapse. She felt as if she had been physically beaten. Adam Francis had seen right into her soul—he'd stripped her of her veneer and her pride, her cool, and the image she tried so hard to maintain. She wanted to hit back at him, but she had nothing to say. She wanted to throw something at him, but she couldn't move. That his words were to keep her awake half the night, and the next night, she had no way of knowing right then. All she felt then was a numbness, not so much because he had told her new things about herself, but because he had seen right through her in the space of a few hours. And *nobody* had done that before.

So what happened now?

She simply didn't know what to say next. It was as if Adam Francis knew her better than she knew herself, and the idea of that was almost terrifying.

Nothing was said for a long time. Jane was confused, bewildered, drained of emotion, and he seemed to be giving her time to absorb what he had said.

Adam Francis spoke first. He waited until he considered the time was right, then he shattered the tension with very carefully chosen words. He kept his tone light as he made it quite clear what he expected of her. 'Okay, since it's my habit to wear clothes while I have dinner, I'll go and get dressed now. You know, I really do hate wearing ties, I wasn't joking, so you won't mind if we eat in here, will you?'

He smiled at her then, and there was no mockery in it. None whatsoever. He was not, contrary to what Jane had thought before meeting him, a totally hard man. She realised at once that he was giving her the chance to start afresh, that this was his way of letting her off the hook.

She looked at him with a new respect, their eyes meeting in understanding, and she trembled slightly. 'I'm not going to apologise, you know.' Her voice was soft now, but it held a note of defiance. 'You must surely see how things looked from my point of view.'

Adam's eyebrows rose in surprise. 'I don't expect anyone to apologise for speaking their mind. As far as I'm concerned, we've cleared the air.'

So he didn't expect an apology. He did not, in fact, expect any comment. Which was just as well, because she was stupid if she'd confirm or deny any of his accusations. She wouldn't give him that satisfaction. It was all far, far too personal.

But there was still the rest of the evening to get through and the unavoidable contact she would have with him during the week ahead. So common sense must prevail. She must meet him halfway. 'Yes, we've cleared the air.' She even managed to smile.

Leaning forward in his chair, Adam looked at her gravely. 'And let's keep it that way. Just be yourself, and for heaven's sake don't worry about my being a client. I want you to speak your mind and be honest with me. You'll find that it makes life much simpler. Now, you haven't given me your answer: do you mind if we have dinner in here?'

'No, I don't mind.'

'Do you realise, now, that you don't have to feel threatened in any way?'

'Yes, I realise that now.'

'So we can *both* relax now?'

She nodded, but just a trifle uncertainly.

'That's not good enough, Jane.' His voice was harsh but a roguish grin broke out on his face. 'Say, "Yes, Adam, we can both relax now." '

A whole host of mixed emotions was rushing around inside Jane, but she laughed in spite of herself. 'Yes, Adam, we can both relax now.'

Adam got to his feet, and the grin changed into an enigmatic smile. 'Then if the lady will excuse me . . .'

Jane leant back in her chair. She was, in fact, a long way from being relaxed. She had never before met anyone even remotely like Adam Francis. He was a fascinating man with the body of an athlete and a mind like a rapier. All this, combined with a great sensitivity and an astonishing perception. For Jane, there were red lights flashing all over the place, danger signals in her mind. She was aware of them, and she would take heed.

Still, her eyes trailed after Adam and rested on the broad and powerful outline of his back as he walked into his bedroom to change.

CHAPTER THREE

'MORE strawberries, Jane?'

'Gosh, no, I've already had two helpings!'

Adam Francis pushed back his chair, stretched out his legs and lit a cigarette. She hadn't seen him smoking before. He picked up the bottle of vintage champagne. 'Then let me fill up your glass.'

Jane hesitated. The bottle was nearly empty and she'd already had more than her fair share of it. 'No, I—I don't think I ought.'

'Ought?' said Adam. 'There's no ought about it. There's no such word, in fact. You like it, don't you?'

'I love it!'

'Then have it!' He emptied the bottle into her glass and Jane giggled, very slightly lightheaded.

'Adam, you're a hedonist!'

'Certainly!' he grinned. 'Is there any other philosophy?'

She laughed at him, unsure whether or not he was serious. 'Do you always drink vintage champagne with your dinner, then?'

'Actually, no. But tonight is special. This is a celebration.'

'Oh, really?' She said it sceptically, unaware that her eyes were sparkling like amber, that the pink flush on her cheeks somehow made her look younger and incredibly vulnerable. 'Of what?'

'Why, meeting you, of course! I've made a new friend.'

Slightly lightheaded or not, Jane was still in control. She was more relaxed than she had been since first setting eyes on Adam, but her guard was still up. It was far too deeply a part of her to be easily dropped. 'We're not friends, we're associates.'

Adam looked heavenward. 'You're a hard woman. I see that it's Winters by name and winters by nature.'

Jane pretended to yawn. 'Spare me!'

'Ah, so I'm not the first man in your life to be treated with such cold disdain. You've heard that line before.'

'You are not "a man in my life". Nor are you my friend. But I'll compromise . . . let's say we're friendly associates.'

Adam appeared to think about that for a moment before shrugging resignedly. 'Well, that's a slight improvement, I suppose.' Then he laughed because Jane was yawning for real. 'Tired?'

'Mmm.'

'Okay, we'd better get the business out of the way. Show me your map of the Birmingham area and I'll tell you what I've got planned.'

'What *you've* got planned?' Jane's eyebrows shot up in astonishment; she was suddenly wide awake. 'I thought I was supposed to make suggestions to you!'

This time his laughter really was infectious—or was it just the champagne? 'I'll get my specs,' she giggled.

'Your what?' He roared with laughter, and Jane pretended to be offended.

'Mr Francis, you have insisted I be myself this evening, so you'll have to put up with me wearing my specs. At this time of night, in this light, I need them.'

'Oh, no, you haven't heard the rest of it yet,' he went on, 'I was just going to get mine!'

The pair of them collapsed with laughter.

'Oh, goodness, they're awful!' Jane tried her best to keep a straight face, but her eyes were twinkling. 'Where on earth did you get those?' He had emerged from his bedroom wearing a dreadful pair of glasses with thick black rims.

'Chicago,' he said haughtily. 'They're the sort that don't break when you sit on them.'

'They're ghastly!'

'I wouldn't call yours glamorous! You could get the feminine version of these, they're very practical.'

'I don't often sit on my specs. Is that another habit of yours?'

'Don't be so cheeky. Get the maps out, woman!'

Jane fetched her briefcase just as the waiter came to clear away the debris of their fabulous dinner. Using the spacious side table, she spread out the map of the area in which Adam wanted to build his next hotel.

When the waiter had left, Adam came over to join her, his hands thrust into his trouser pockets as his eyes travelled over the papers in front of him. He'd changed. His glasses no longer seemed funny, and the laughter had been dispensed with, for both of them. Suddenly he was more like the man Jane had originally imagined him to be: intense and concerned only with his next project. He was no longer Adam Francis the charming host, he was Adam Francis the property magnate.

'So what has John Brinkman come up with?'

Jane watched him as he concentrated on the sketches in front of him. What she had to say was so well rehearsed she hardly needed to think about it.

She was looking at him in profile, the straight nose, the generous mouth, no longer smiling; the eyes no longer lit with amusement but still—always—lit with intensity. How green they were!

But the feature which most plainly told of his determination and hardness as far as business was concerned was his jawline. It was set now, stern, unyielding. Had Jane been looking at him then for the very first time, she'd never have suspected him to have a good sense of humour, to be capable of laughing so openly and so easily.

She picked up a pencil and pointed towards an area outlined in red. 'Mr Brinkman thinks this would make a good site for your hotel. It's a little farther out of town than the original site and it covers a slightly smaller area, but that wouldn't be a problem—you could build the hotel one storey higher or have an underground car park instead of having one at the rear. The land isn't on the market. A good slice of it is owned by a transport company who are having financial difficulties. Mr Brinkman thinks they'd sell without much persuasion. However, there is one problem . . .'

Jane pinpointed a place on the map which ran alongside the land owned by the transport company. 'This stretch here is owned by the people living there. It's a row of terraced houses and the occupants each own the freehold. It should be easy enough to buy these people out—except for one couple. They are Mr and Mrs Clement, living right in the centre of the row. They're elderly, late sixties perhaps, and they're categorically not interested in selling. But Mr Brinkman thinks if they were offered enough, they'd move out. It seems the old fellow has recently been ill, and they don't want the upheaval; either that, or they have some sort of emotional attachment to the place.'

Jane faltered slightly, acutely aware of Adam's nearness as he leant further over the table, standing uncomfortably close to her. She caught the faint, earthy smell of his aftershave and the freshly laundered smell of the shirt he'd put on after his shower. His mane of dark blond hair looked slightly wild; it was brushed back carelessly, apart from one lock which had fallen over his forehead as he bent. It was straight but for a few slight curls at the base of his neck, where it was just a little too long. Oh, but it suited him. It was a magnificent head of hair and Jane had a sudden, ridiculous urge to touch it.

She moved away from him slightly. 'Of course, this old couple might think very differently if Francisco Enterprises acquired the rest of the land. In fact, all the householders would be very much persuaded to sell if they thought there was going to be a lot of demolition and rebuilding going on next door to them. They have no way of knowing how much you want all the land, for the size of hotel you want to build. It could bring the price of all the little houses down considerably, if you put that sort of pressure on them.'

Adam drew up a chair and sat down. 'You've done a good bit of research there. Tell John thanks. Thank you, too. However, I'm not interested. Something else has come up which is far more suitable. Now, I've found out about this place which is some miles further out, slightly to the east . . .' He pointed to an area at the top end of the map. 'We can just about see it here.'

'But you gave us a specific radius! You said——'

'Oh, yes,' he said. 'I'm not criticising.' He held up his large, square hand on which the nails were white and short, immaculate. 'I gave you explicit instructions and you came up with an alternative. Fair enough . . .'

Jane was interested to hear about this other land he had in mind. She was also interested, and gratified, to note that Adam was speaking to her now absolutely as his equal. She had been completely wrong in her earlier assumptions about him. He did not let her age, sex, or anything else interfere or distract him when it came to business. He was speaking to her then as coldly and brusquely as he had many times on the telephone. Wasting no words and keeping right to the point.

'I've changed my mind,' he explained. 'I'd be prepared to go farther out in this case because the site is very convenient for the motorway. Look. There's an exit here. It would be a good stopping place for business people, commercial travellers, and so on. There's easy access to the Exhibition Centre, it's near enough to the town centre but far enough away that people could avoid town centre traffic. They could be on their way and bypass Birmingham completely, if that's what they'd prefer. It's also near enough to get the overflow from the airport hotel. In fact, it's eminently suitable.'

Jane nodded. He was right, of course. Of course! 'Is the land up for sale?' she asked.

He smiled slightly. 'It's being auctioned on Wednesday.'

'This Wednesday?'

'Mm. And you're going to buy it for me.'

'Me? Oh, I don't think I——' It was a worrying thought. Jane had no experience whatever of land auctions.

'Well, obviously I can't go personally. If there were a whisper that Francisco Enterprises is interested, the price would go up. But nobody will recognise you, or know who you're representing. I'll get it a darn sight cheaper if you do the bidding. I'll brief you, don't worry.'

'All right.' Mr Brinkman was haunting her again: If there's anything else Adam wants you to do for him, he'd said, please give him top priority.

'It's a pity about the original site, though,' Adam went on. 'Those high-minded petty officials!'

Jane smiled inwardly. Mr Brinkman had predicted

that remark, and he'd been precisely right! 'So you're absolutely not interested in our alternative?'

'No. Besides, it isn't my style to shove people out of their homes in order to build a hotel.'

It pleased Jane to hear that. So he was a man of principle, too. How many more times would she be surprised by him?

He folded up the papers for her and she put them back into her briefcase, glancing at her watch as she did so. 'Heavens, it's almost one o'clock! Adam, would you ring down to the porter, please, and have him call a taxi for me. I'm ready to leave.'

'No way.'

Puzzled, she looked up at him. What very clear eyes he had, really quite beautiful. And they spoke volumes, when he chose to let them. They were smiling now. The business man had been replaced by the host.

'I shall take you home personally.'

'Oh, there's no need. In fact it's silly——'

'Johnstone's left the keys to the Rolls in reception,' he said. 'And a proper young lady like you must be accompanied home in the proper way.'

She narrowed her eyes. 'Getting at me again, are you?'

There was no hesitation. 'No, not this time, as it happens. There is a certain amount of propriety which is desirable when one is dealing with a lady such as you.'

'A lady such as me?' She was still unsure whether he was teasing her.

'A lady. Just . . . a lady.' He paused as if he had been going to add something else, but thought better of it. Then, changing the serious mood of the moment, he grinned wickedly. 'You need looking after.'

'Oh!' All her indignation was in that single sound. He'd said that just to annoy her, knowing how independent and capable she was. If he'd been

standing any closer, she'd have poked him in the ribs.
She had to make do with pulling a face at him.

'Some lady!' he grinned.

'It wasn't a bad evening after all, eh, Jane?'

'It was a lovely evening, thank you.' They'd pulled
up outside the building where she lived.

'Oh, you're just saying that because I'm a client.' He
was teasing her, but Jane hardly heard him. She could
see at a glance that the living room light of their flat
was still on. Gerald! Oh, she should have phoned him
when it got to midnight, she really should ... How
thoughtless of her, her father must be worrying about
her ...

Then, very slowly, Adam said her name. He leaned
over from the driving seat and for one dreadful,
thrilling, panic-stricken moment, Jane thought he was
going to kiss her. He clicked the lock on her side of the
door. 'It locks automatically when you get in,' he
explained. He said nothing else for the moment, but
Jane knew from the smile hovering around his lips
that he had read her thoughts, seen her panic. In that
instant she resented him intensely, because he had
teased her deliberately, but mainly because she
resented being read so easily. Nobody else could do it,
so how come he could?

'Goodnight, Adam.'

'No invitation for coffee?'

'No.' She said it firmly, very firmly. Being herself
and acting friendly towards him was one thing, but
taking a client home for coffee, even in the presence of
her father, was really quite another! It would be just
too friendly.

'Well—er—a hot milky drink, then?'

'You're hardly the Ovaltine type!'

'Really,' on a serious note, 'do you think you know
what type I am? After one evening?'

'I know enough to . . .' No, she couldn't finish that sentence. She couldn't tell him she knew enough to realise she must avoid him like the plague. But she couldn't avoid him for the coming week . . . Dammit! '*Goodnight*, Adam.'

He got out of the car and held the door open for her.

'What time will you call at the office tomorrow?'

'Not so fast! Come on.' He got hold of her hand and she stiffened.

'What are you doing?' she demanded.

'I'm seeing you home.'

'I am home!'

'To your front door, silly.'

'Oh, Adam, this is ridiculous!' She didn't want this, she didn't want him taking her right up to her front door. Her father was waiting up for her, and she didn't want to give him reason to start asking questions. Bless him, he'd be sure to pull her leg about it.

They reached her front door and Jane fumbled for her key, using delaying tactics and waiting for him to go. Damn the man, why didn't he just go now! She never found her key. The door swung open and there stood her father, smiling.

'I thought I heard your footsteps, darling . . . Ah, we have a visitor! How nice!'

It was typical of Gerald to greet someone like that, even a total stranger. That was the type of person Gerald was. He loved having visitors, he always had, and these days they didn't have so many . . .

Jane sighed inwardly, resignedly, knowing what would happen next. Oh, how very dear her father was—but she wished he hadn't waited up for her! Her eyes swept over his face with concern, but he looked all right. A little tired, perhaps, but he wasn't in any discomfort.

Gerald stepped forward, reaching out his hand to

meet that of Adam Francis. 'How very good of you to bring Jane home, Mr——'

'Adam.'

'Adam. I'm Gerald—Gerald Winters, Jane's father.'

'I'm very pleased to meet you, Gerald.'

The two men shook hands vigorously while Jane stood there like an onlooker, not at all involved with the introductions!

Gerald stepped back into the hallway. 'Come in, Adam. Have a cup of coffee, won't you?'

'I will indeed. Thank you!'

With her back to her father, Jane turned to Adam Francis, a look of outrage on her face. Since her father was in earshot, and would wonder what on earth had got into her, she couldn't speak her mind. She had to make do with the filthy look she was giving.

Adam looked at her innocently and shrugged nonchalantly, as if all this had been out of his control, when Jane knew full well he had engineered it! She was not amused. Why Adam Francis should be so curious to meet her father, and to see where she lived, she had no idea. Perhaps he was just too nosey for his own good.

Adam seated himself on the sofa and Gerald settled into his big armchair near the fire. Jane didn't bother sitting. She flung her bag on to the sofa, at the side of her guest, and dropped her briefcase on the floor. 'How are you, Daddy? Did you eat tonight?'

'Yes, yes, I'm fine, darling.' Gerald smiled at her concern.

'I'll put the kettle on,' she said, with a pointed look at Adam.

He pretended not to notice her irritation. 'I'm sorry we're so late,' he said to Gerald, as Jane left the room, 'it's that daughter of yours—she talks too much.'

'Oh, I know that!'

That was all Jane heard. She slammed the kitchen

door deliberately and went about making the coffee. What a cheek! And Gerald had no idea he was being facetious—as far as he was concerned, Jane did talk a lot. But then she did talk a lot—with Gerald.

Just what was Adam Francis up to? He'd put her in her place well and truly much earlier in the evening. What was he trying to prove now? That he could get the better of her again? That he could control her, even? To a certain extent he could, of course, inasmuch as he was a client and she had certain obligations to him. But accepting Gerald's invitation when he knew Jane was tired, and she had refused him coffee, was taking liberties. She would simply have to make another stand with this man, establish boundary lines. Lines which absolutely must not be crossed again.

Dropping one of her best coffee mugs and smashing it to pieces did not make Jane's mood any better. Those mixed emotions came into play again, rushing around inside her as she busied herself in the kitchen. How could she possibly feel so many things about Adam Francis ... things which were so much at variance with each other? She was annoyed by him, respected him, resented him, amused by him, puzzled, impressed and—oh, really!

When she emerged from the kitchen, her father and Adam were chatting away as if they'd known each other for years. They were talking engineering—right up her father's street! Oh, he'd probably sit there for hours ...

She plonked the tray on the side table and waited for a chance to interrupt them. She didn't get that chance. Wordlessly she poured out the coffee and let them get on with it.

'You're not English, are you, Adam?' Gerald asked at length.

Jane had almost fallen asleep. She'd given up

looking daggers at Adam when her eyes started to droop.

'I'm Brazilian,' Adam smiled. 'Born in Rio of a Brazilian mother and an American father. These days my home—or rather my base—is in New York. But I move around quite a lot.'

'Brazilian, eh? Why, my wife and I spent part of our honeymoon in Brazil! Actually, we toured round quite a bit. Moira had always wanted to see South America, and I'd inherited a few hundred from an aunt of mine. Mind you, we didn't go by jumbo jet in those days! My wife loved it. She was Scottish, did I mention that before . . .?'

And that gave rise to another half hour's conversation. Gerald missed his wife terribly, would talk about her at the slightest prompting, and Adam Francis was giving him plenty of that.

By the time Adam finally got to his feet, Jane was absolutely seething. 'Well, thanks for your hospitality, Gerald,' he said smoothly. 'No, don't get up. I'm sure Jane won't mind seeing me out.'

'It'll be my pleasure!' said Jane, with deliberate ambiguity. She saw her father's puzzled look as she struggled to her feet. She was shattered. 'What time will you call at the office tomorrow?'

'I won't be calling at the office tomorrow.'

For an instant, Jane was relieved—until she remembered the auction. 'But the land auction's on Wednesday! When are you going to brief me on that?'

'In the evening, of course.' He smiled down at her, a slow smile with just a touch of insolence about it. 'Over dinner.'

Jane's eyes flashed with anger, then narrowed suspiciously.

'I'm spending the day with my architects tomorrow,' Adam went on, his tone slightly bored but ever so reasonable. 'So I'm afraid I'll have to steal another of your evenings.'

She was still suspicious. It wasn't as if he had to go out of town tomorrow; his architects were in the City, just a few streets away from Brinkman's. 'Well, couldn't we meet at lunchtime? Or perhaps I could walk round to the architect's? I mean, it won't take long to brief me, will it?'

They were standing in the middle of the living room, with Gerald looking on and getting more puzzled by the minute.

'I'm sorry,' said Adam, not looking at all sorry, 'I'll be tied up all day. We'll have to meet in the evening. Er—did you have other plans for tomorrow night?'

Gerald, who could stand it no longer, chipped in then. 'Jane, this is business!' He looked at his daughter as if she'd gone mad. 'If Adam's tied up all day—well, you'll just have to postpone your date with Paul. You must have dinner with Adam!'

'Paul?' Adam's quizzical look was directed straight at Jane, but it was Gerald who answered.

'Paul Meekins. The junior partner from the office.'

'I see.'

'Please say goodnight now, Daddy,' Jane said hastily, 'I'm awfully tired.' She moved quickly towards the door. She couldn't blame her father for making a perfectly innocent remark but—oh Lord, why did he have to say that? Cancelling her date with Paul posed no problem at all, since it was only a figment of her imagination! But things were getting a bit tricky and she had to get rid of Adam Francis quickly, before Gerald told him anything else!

'Goodnight, Adam.' Gerald still looked nonplussed. 'It was nice meeting you.'

'Same here. I'll see you again soon.'

No doubt meaning tomorrow night, thought Jane. Well, that's what he thinks! I might be obliged to have dinner with him, but the evening will be as brief as I can possibly make it. And there's *no way* he'll end up chatting to my father again! She'd have Adam pick her up in town tomorrow, and when he brought her home she'd make damn certain he didn't get invited in for coffee.

She was very careful to close the living room door behind Adam as he stepped into the hall. It was not a big flat and she didn't want to risk her father overhearing what she said to him. 'About our meeting tomorrow,' she said hurriedly, opening the front door as she spoke, 'I'm planning to work until seven because I've so much to catch up with while Mr Brinkman's away. So may I suggest you pick me up outside the building at seven o'clock?'

Adam nodded. Then, with the familiar mockery in his eyes, he said, 'So they've made young Meekins a junior partner, eh? Is that what appeals to you, Jane? The smart young executive type?'

Jane had anticipated some such remark and was ready with her answer. It would have been very nice to let Adam think she had something going with Paul; it would make him think he'd been wrong in his earlier accusations. But she couldn't do it because if Adam called at the office later that week, and happened to see Paul, he might just make a comment to the younger man. She wouldn't put it past him. And if that happened, she'd have some very awkward explaining to do! Inevitably she'd end up looking a fool in both men's eyes.

So she kept her tone absolutely neutral. 'Don't jump to conclusions. I've worked in the same firm as Paul for over a year and we're just friends.'

'So is this the first date you've made with him?'

'That,' she said coldly, 'really is none of your business.'

It did the trick. Adam made no retort. But he didn't make a move, either. Rather, he stood looking down at her from his superior height, his clear eyes giving no indication of what was going through his mind. Suddenly, in an attitude of confidentiality, he nodded his head in the direction of the living room and whispered, 'Are you sure that man in there is your father?'

Dear heaven, he was incorrigible! Didn't he take anything seriously? It seemed that no matter what she said, she couldn't rattle him.

'Go on,' she said in a bored voice, 'out with it. What are you going to say now?'

'Oh, not much,' he said innocently. 'It just seems so strange. I mean, Gerald's so friendly and natural and hospitable. It's hard to believe you're related, let alone father and daughter!'

Drawing herself up to her full height, Jane met his gaze squarely. 'Since you invited me to speak my mind and be absolutely honest with you, hear this: you are the most insolent, arrogant, facetious and irritating man I've ever met!'

Adam leaned against the door-jamb, nodding each time she came out with a new adjective. 'Tomorrow night should be interesting, then.'

She wanted to hit him. 'You know very well I don't want to have dinner with you tomorrow. And I don't believe for one minute you couldn't spare me half an hour during the day. You've got me in a very awkward position, and well you know it. You've won, but you needn't look so smug about it. You've won only because you're an important client.'

He smiled, reaching out to touch her cheek before she even guessed what was coming. He traced the outline of her jaw with his fingers, looking into her eyes with a gaze that was suddenly, startlingly serious—and almost frighteningly cold. 'Oh, no, Jane, being a client has little to do with it. I've won because I always get what I want.'

And then he was gone.

For long seconds Jane leaned against the closed door, trying desperately to make some sense of the emotions churning inside her, trying desperately to make sense of Adam Francis. Unconsciously her hands came up to touch her burning cheeks. What did he mean by his last remark? What was it, exactly, that he wanted of her?

She went back into the living room, too tired and too confused to think straight.

'What a thoroughly nice chap!' Gerald declared.

Jane sighed inwardly. 'That's hardly the way I'd describe him.'

It was as if she hadn't spoken. 'He's a big fellow, isn't he? Must be six foot two if he's an inch!'

'I suppose so.' She was gathering up the coffee mugs.

'Good-looking, too, eh?'

'I didn't notice.'

'Jane!'

Turning to face her father, she couldn't help laughing at the look on his face. 'Oh, I suppose so.'

'But I just don't understand you, my girl.' Gerald was suddenly agitated. 'Why the devil were you so rude to him?'

'I wasn't rude, I——'

'I mean, how did you have the nerve, when he's a client? In any case, he was so likeable, I couldn't see any reason for rudeness! And why were you so reluctant to have dinner with him, especially since it's business?'

Jane's eyes closed involuntarily. She was almost swaying on her feet. 'Daddy, I'm exhausted. You don't understand. Adam and I . . .' Oh, how on earth could she put this? 'We—we established a sort of working relationship tonight. He—well, he sort of sensed my nervousness and told me to forget that he's a client. He told me I should just be myself.'

'I see.' Gerald's face fell. He suddenly looked as tired as she felt. 'And being yourself made you put up all the barriers, of course.'

'What do you mean by that?'

'Oh, come on, Jane,' he said wearily. 'It's taken you a long time to get over Billy, to start going out again. And so far, there's only been the occasional date with Paul. Paul's obviously not the man who's going to make you forget Billy ever existed. But Adam Francis might be. I think you've already got an inkling of this, and you're frightened by it.'

'That's absolutely ridiculous!'

'Jane——'

'Please—I'm tired. Let's not discuss him any further.' Feeling instantly guilty for raising her voice, she went over to Gerald and hugged him tightly. 'I'm sorry, Pop. But don't get carried away with silly ideas just because you happened to like Adam.'

Gerald put his arms around her, resting her head against his shoulder and smoothing her hair, as he used to when she was little. Did a father ever stop worrying about his daughter, no matter what her age? If only Moira were here; things would be so different for Jane if her mother were alive. Jane felt too much responsibility for him, and it worried him terribly. She tried so hard to be everything to her father: provider, daughter, companion, and she just wasn't getting on with her own life.

But Gerald Winters had seen something very encouraging tonight, very encouraging indeed. He was sixty years old and an extremely good judge of character. No, he decided, he wouldn't warn Jane that she must never, ever, make the mistake of under-estimating Adam Francis. He would just let things take their course. 'All right, darling,' he said quietly, 'we won't discuss him any more.'

Adam Francis settled comfortably in the winged armchair in the sitting room of his hotel suite. London was sleeping, Park Lane was silent, but the lateness of the hour was as nothing to him. His mind was razor-sharp, his body fully relaxed. He looked out at the black, starless sky in brooding deliberation, letting his mind run over the evening's events, knowing from many years of experience that he would find a solution to the problem he was faced with.

By the age of four he'd been fatherless, by nine he was motherless. But from sixteen onwards he had mastered all his problems, alone, rising by his own skills from the depths of poverty to the zenith of success. At twenty-three he had made his first million, and now . . .

Now, at thirty-seven, his business life left nothing to be desired. He had achieved all he had set out to achieve, and more. The world of commerce no longer presented a challenge to him; he had mastered it until, now, his business dealings were hardly more than an entertaining hobby.

Could Jane Winters really be described as a problem? Wouldn't mystery be a better word? A slow smile spread across his lips as he thought of her. Jane, the beautiful creature who had walked into his life a few short hours ago. Jane, the woman who had brought a breath of fresh air into the life of one who was world-weary. He wanted her! Jane, so serious, so intense . . . with all her barriers and inhibitions . . .

He relived the moment of their meeting at the airport. The impact of that meeting had rendered him momentarily speechless. At first he had thought he knew her, that she was someone he had met before. But that wasn't so, because he wouldn't, couldn't have forgotten if he'd met Jane Winters in the past. That face! Her face was unforgettable. She was beautiful, she didn't know how beautiful, with her flawless, translucent skin, her light, tawny eyes; almond-shaped eyes which held flecks of gold, shaded under thick, dark lashes. In his mind's eye he could see that face now as clearly as he had when he had been standing only inches away from her.

At first he had thought she was nervous, perhaps because it was her task to entertain him. He had made every effort to be casual, to put her at her ease, but it hadn't worked. In the silence of his room he laughed aloud at the memory of her outburst, when she had finally voiced her thoughts and let him know how she disapproved of his behaviour. How entertaining that had been! How beautiful she had looked with the light dancing on her angry eyes, and her elegant, slender hands waving about as she let him have it!

More importantly, that scene had been very informative. The impression he had gained of her in the car had been confirmed, and then some. She was very much on the defensive, even afraid of him. He could understand that better now. Jane was not yet aware of what had happened tonight. She was determined to resist him every inch of the way . . . Yes, he did have a problem on his hands.

Hyde Park stirred to life with the dawn chorus. Adam looked at his watch. It was six a.m. It was still dark, and for the moment he didn't know what he should do. His plans would have to be changed, of course. Completely changed. He got up and refilled his glass.

He would have to play his cards very carefully. He must take care not to frighten her off. Softly, softly catchee Jane Winters! Above all else Adam was an expert when it came to human nature. His outrageous lie had been justified. He had told Jane she was not his type finally to put her at her ease. Dear heaven, he'd never seen anyone so genuinely uptight. And, as far as women were concerned, he had known them all: the coy, the shy, the promiscuous, the would-be manipulators, the fortune-hunters, the husband-seekers; older and younger, rich, poor, beautiful, plain . . .

Jane Winters was like an unopened flower. A rosebud tightly closed, hiding its beauty from the world because of its fear to open up and shine. Why was she like that? *Why?* Meeting Gerald and seeing her flat had told him only that she lived modestly with a father she obviously adored. That, and the amusing titbit about young Meekins. But Paul Meekins was no problem to Adam. It was Jane who had the problem. It was something rooted very deeply within her. Already he had several theories as to what it might be. In time, he would find out.

When daylight flooded the room, Adam Francis knew precisely what he had to do. He phoned the airport. He showered and changed, and in the remaining minutes before Johnstone was due, he phoned his sister in Brazil. He wanted to tell someone, and for the time being his sister was the only person he could tell.

'Carmen? Hold tight and listen, I have wonderful news. I'm getting married . . . No, there's nothing wrong with the line . . . Yes, you heard me correctly . . . Oh, let's say five or six weeks. A couple of months at the most . . . I can't tell you the date, because the lady concerned doesn't know about it yet . . . No, I haven't gone crazy. What? . . . But my dear, you know I just wouldn't take no for an answer!'

CHAPTER FOUR

IN the cold light of day the answer was remarkably simple. Jane had done a great deal of thinking during the night, but, on waking, her mind had presented her with the only logical conclusion.

Not surprisingly she had overslept that morning. Her alarm had rung, but she hadn't even heard it. It was eleven-fifteen by the time she got to the office and she was still sitting there, staring blankly out of the window. The cover was on her typewriter, the post stacked on her desk in a neat pile; she hadn't even taken her jacket off.

It had been past three when she had finally got to bed, and turned six before she went to sleep. She had been unable to get Adam Francis out of her mind.

She still couldn't.

Chemistry, that was the answer. One word was all it took to explain the impact he'd had on her. In her college days and in her office life, she had heard girls talking about physical attraction; she'd read about it, she'd seen it acted out in films, but never before had she experienced it for herself. Acknowledging it didn't make it any easier to understand, though.

They called it chemistry, but did that necessarily mean it worked both ways, or could one person feel it while the other didn't? Adam had told her categorically that she wasn't his type—yet he had manoeuvred her into spending another evening with him. Why?

For the first time in her life she regretted her lack of experience. It seemed ridiculous that she could have reached the age of twenty-three and not know the answer to these questions. But she had nothing to relate to, nothing to compare this physical attraction with. She had never felt this with Billy, nothing even remotely like it, nor with the few young men she had dated prior to getting involved with Billy. So what exactly was this thing called physical attraction?

During her hours of sleeplessness Jane had tried very hard to convince herself that she didn't like Adam Francis, but it just hadn't worked. She'd realised that her reactions, all her reactions to Adam were not what they ought to be. What he had told her about herself hadn't exactly been news to her; what she had resented was his ability to read her as nobody else had done. But later, perversely, she had felt an overwhelming respect for him because of his very ability.

Also, the anger she had felt at him wheedling his way into her home had gone by the time she got into bed. In retrospect his persistence had served only to amuse her. Ridiculous though it was, she had even admired his audacity in manipulating her. How could one help feeling admiration for a man so shrewd, so positive, who always gets what he wants from life?

Then, just before drifting into sleep, she had cursed Adam Francis aloud, wondering how one evening with one man could make her feel so frighteningly unsettled.

On waking, however, her mind had presented her with the only logical conclusion. The chaos of her thoughts had been sorted out and the answer was as clear as the morning's cold autumn sky. What she felt for Adam Francis was merely physical attraction—a strong sexual pull. There was nothing more to it than that.

'Jane?'

Startled, she turned from the window to find Paul Meekins standing in her office.

'Are you all right?' He frowned. Her pale skin looked even paler this morning. In fact, she looked positively upset.

'Yes, Paul, yes. I—I overslept, that's all.' She quickly picked up her letter-opener and reached for the stack of envelopes on her desk. Paul moved closer, watching her curiously. He'd never seen her like this before. She was a bundle of nerves. 'Conscientious though you are, I can't imagine you're upset because you came into work late. What's wrong, Jane?'

'Nothing's wrong!' she snapped at him, then apologised immediately. 'It's just that I have a lot to do and I hate being late.'

'I see.' He returned her smile and played things her way. No doubt her boy-friend was the cause of this, but it was more than he dared do to pry. 'Adam Francis came in this morning,' he went on. 'Actually, I found him sitting in my office when I arrived. Eight-thirty on the dot!'

'Oh, yes?' Jane's voice was nonchalant, trying to hide even from herself the fact that the news, the very mention of Adam's name, affected her.

'He's had to leave the country,' Paul informed her then, 'and he asked me to——'

'Leave the country?' The nonchalance was gone. 'But ...' She was at a loss to understand, but she covered for it quickly. 'But he has business to attend to tomorrow! That is, we were—I mean, I was going to——'

'Don't worry about that.' Paul held up a reassuring hand. 'He's briefed me on the Birmingham business. He asked me to go and do the bidding for him. He said you wouldn't mind, that he'd asked you to do it, but you weren't keen on the idea. And you weren't here to confer with, so he's instructed me instead. He asked me to apologise to you for his sudden absence, but he's got an emergency on his hands. He said something had come up which he couldn't possibly have anticipated.'

'Well, rather you than me,' Jane said lightly, relieved that she didn't have to go to Birmingham, relieved that she didn't have to have dinner with Adam, relieved that he'd left the country. 'I've never been to an auction in my life.'

'There's nothing to it.' Paul laughed. 'Especially in this case. Mr Francis wants that land and he told me to keep on bidding until I get it. Mind you——' He broke off, stroking his chin thoughtfully as if something terrible had just occurred to him. 'Yes, I think I'll drive up there tonight. The auction doesn't start till eleven, but you never know . . . The traffic on the motorway could be heavy, and if I were late—well, that doesn't bear thinking about, does it? I'll be on the safe side and stay in Birmingham tonight.'

Paul's words brought a sudden flush to Jane's cheeks as she remembered that as far as Adam was concerned, Paul would have been able, now, to take her out. Apparently he hadn't made any comment to Paul. But she had to make sure. 'Er—did Mr Francis say anything else? What I mean is, did you tell him you'd be staying in Birmingham tonight?'

'No.' He looked at her strangely. She didn't seem to be listening properly. 'The idea's only just occurred to me.' Why was she so preoccupied, anxious? For purely selfish reasons, Paul hoped that her boy-friend was the cause of this, that something had gone wrong. If Jane ever needed a shoulder to cry on, he would be standing first in line.

'So he didn't make any other comment?'

'Only that he wanted you to ring his architects and cancel his appointment. But don't worry, I did that at nine o'clock.'

'Thanks, Paul.' Jane smiled so warmly then that Paul thought he'd actually made some progress with her.

'Jane——'

'Yes?'

'Oh . . . nothing. I—I'll see you later in the week.' He turned away from her, but Jane quickly called him back. Illogically, she was feeling generous towards Paul just then. She had been using him, though he didn't know it, and nothing had been said to precipitate an embarrassing situation. Again illogically, she was giving Paul credit for that. All she really cared about was that she hadn't been found out.

'What were you going to say? Have you got something on your mind?'

But Paul's nerve had deserted him. He had had so many frosty refusals from Jane that it had acted like aversion therapy. He was very wary of asking her out again. Besides, she probably hadn't finished with her boy-friend; more likely it was just a lovers' tiff. 'No.' He shrugged. 'I've forgotten what I was going to say, actually. See you.'

So! Within the space of ten minutes Jane's life had righted itself. Everything was all right again—simple, straightforward, *safe*—and her feeling of relief was enormous. Adam Francis had left the country! With luck it would be another year before he needed to make a personal visit to Brinkman's. From now on he would be just another voice on the telephone. She had no need to wonder any more about—well, about anything! All she had to do now was to forget him.

Jane threw herself into her work. She kept right on top of things at the office, wanting to have everything up to date for her boss's return. At home she caught up with the housework, getting rid of the ironing and cleaning the flat until it sparkled. But by Friday she was forced to acknowledge that forgetting Adam was proving to be much harder than she had expected.

Being settled in the safety of routine was not the same as being settled within herself, as she was before she had met Adam. She told herself that her surroundings were to blame, that being at work made her think of Francisco Enterprises, which in turn made her think of Adam. It wasn't as if Adam had phoned her, though. He had spoken to Paul, but not to her. In Mr Brinkman's absence, Paul was dealing with the Francisco Enterprises documents and he gave the relevant typing to his own secretary. Still, Jane blamed her surroundings for the fact that Adam was constantly in her thoughts. She was sure that being at home over the weekend would help to push him from her mind once and for all.

'Mr Brinkman! Good morning, I'm pleased to see you. You're looking well. Did you have a good holiday?' It was nine o'clock on Monday morning. Jane had just arrived, picked up her shorthand notebook and gone straight in to see her boss.

'Yes, thank you.'

His short answer told her immediately that something was bothering him. 'Jane, I tried to ring you at home this morning but your father said you'd just left. I've been here since eight, and the first thing that happened was a telephone call from our illustrious client.'

'Mr Francis?' Jane sat down opposite her boss, notebook and pencil at the ready, appalled at the way her stomach contracted involuntarily. During the weekend, she had not achieved what she'd hoped to achieve. She had taken her father to the cinema; they'd had a few laughs over a game of cards that went on for four hours. Their next-door neighbour, Mrs Graham, who normally spent Sundays at her son's home, had invited them to dinner. Her son had gone on holiday and Mrs Graham claimed that she hadn't made a 'proper' Sunday dinner for more than five years, since her husband died. She had been grateful for the company of Gerald and his daughter, and Jane had been grateful for the distraction. But despite being away from the office, and keeping herself very busy, she had not succeeded in forgetting Adam. Now, the very mention of his name was making her stomach turn inside out.

'Who else?' said Mr Brinkman. 'He wants the documents relating to his purchase of the Birmingham plot. Paul got everything tied up quickly, so there's no problem. Adam's a wily old devil, isn't he? Didn't I tell you he always finds a way——' He broke off, waving an impatient hand as if he were cross with himself for getting sidetracked. 'Anyway, Adam wants the papers today.'

Jane looked at him curiously, at a loss to understand his obvious anxiety. 'All right. I'll see that they're in the post.'

'No, Jane! I said he wants them today. He wants you to deliver them to him straight away.'

'All right.' She said it calmly, but her stomach tightened even further at the news that Adam was back in town. A meeting would be inevitable, therefore, unless—'I'll send them over by taxi, if you don't mind. I mean, now you're back, we'll be busy today . . .'

Her voice trailed off at the expression on John Brinkman's face. It was a mixture of amusement and irritation.

'Let me explain,' he said hastily. 'Mr Francis wants you personally to deliver the papers. You obviously got on well with him last week. We can't use a courier service and we certainly can't use a taxi! He's at home, you see.'

The remark meant nothing to Jane at first. 'Oh!' she said, horrified. 'You mean he's in his New York apartment!'

'No. He's at *home*, at his private retreat in the Caribbean.'

'The Caribbean? I didn't know——'

'Not many people do.' Mr Brinkman cut her off. 'You're very honoured to be invited,' he added wryly. 'Sorry, Jane, but you have to leave immediately—like now! That's why I phoned you. I wanted to avoid your coming into the office. I was going to send Paul to your home with the papers, then you could've left straight away.'

Jane leapt to her feet, filled with an inexplicable panic. 'But this is ridiculous! What's his hurry?'

'Heaven knows,' Mr. Brinkman shrugged, 'but nothing he does surprises me any more.'

'I can't go.'

Her boss looked at her as if she'd gone mad. 'Jane, we're talking about our most valued client. If he wants to spend hundreds of pounds to ensure a personal delivery service, who are we to refuse him?' He went on, cutting her off with a sharp look as she opened her mouth to protest. 'Your ticket will be waiting at the British Airways desk at Heathrow. You will fly to Barbados via Antigua. From Barbados you will sail to San Pablo, where Mr Francis' house is. He said he'd have someone pick you up at Barbados airport.'

Seeing the look of despair on her face, he smiled suddenly. 'My dear, it's not such a terrible prospect! The Caribbean is very lovely and I'm sure Adam will make the perfect host . . .'

'I don't want to go! I can't. You see—it's my father. He's not well at the moment.' It was the truth, of course. But neither Mr Brinkman nor anyone else in the office knew about Gerald's condition, so that was as much as Jane could say.

'Jane, what on earth is the matter with you? I spoke to your father this morning, remember? He sounded perfectly well to me. In fact, he said it would be lovely

for you to spend a couple of days abroad, with Mr
Francis. Now, Jane, will you just get out of here——'

Trust Gerald! Oh, he would think it a lovely idea,
wouldn't he? Adam Francis had scored a big hit with
Gerald!

'But there's my work ...' Jane's protests were
getting weaker and weaker. If she didn't go, she'd
have her father to contend with.

Mr Brinkman put a stop to her nonsense with two
sharp sentences. 'If I need help in the office I'll
engage a temp. Stop wasting time, and remember that
we're all paid to carry out our clients' instructions.' He
thrust a small white envelope across the desk at her.
'There's some cash in there, which should be plenty to
cover the needs of your journey. Sign here for it,
please.'

Before Jane could say anything else he picked up the
telephone. 'Paul? Would you bring the papers in here,
please. Jane's ready to leave now.'

It was three hours later, when the jumbo jet was
thundering upwards from Heathrow airport, that Jane
finally had a chance to catch her breath. She was
sitting in the window seat in the half-empty, luxurious
first-class section of the aircraft. So Adam had
instructed that she travel first class! He must have,
because Mr Brinkman would never have ordered a
first-class seat when it cost so much more than
economy class.

Jane looked down at the ticket, still clutched in her
hand, and frowned suspiciously. It was an open-ended
ticket, which meant that no date had been set for her
return. Why was that? Just what had Adam Francis
said to Mr Brinkman? She sighed impatiently. It
didn't really matter. She had no intention of spending
any unnecessary time in Adam's company. She would
deliver the papers, get the necessary signature, then
get the first plane ...

The thought trailed off as she remembered Gerald's amusement that morning. When Jane dashed into their flat, having left a taxi outside with its meter ticking over, her father's first words were an expression of delight that Jane was going to see Adam Francis again.

Jane had ignored the remark and headed straight for her bedroom, her father on her heels. She started rummaging through her drawers, looking for her passport. 'Daddy, Mr Adam Francis is putting me to all this trouble just so he can sign a few lousy papers for his lousy piece of land for his next lousy hotel!'

Gerald perched on the side of her bed and smiled up at her, amused at her flushed face and angry eyes. 'I wonder why he's doing that?' he said drolly.

'Because he's power-mad, that's why!' She found her passport, stuffed it into her handbag, pulled her overnight case from the wardrobe and flung it on the bed. 'And it just goes to show how spoiled the man is, if he can have people running around for him like this!'

'But he's rich, darling, he can afford to be pandered to. You can't condemn someone just because——'

'Never mind that! Why couldn't we have used a courier? We've done that in the past when he's wanted things urgently. Why did he insist I personally take his precious papers?'

'I wonder.'

Jane was busy throwing a few clothes into her suitcase. Just one change of clothing. 'Now listen, Daddy. If you're unwell, please phone me.'

'Of course, darling. Have you got the number?'

'The——? Oh, hell, no. But Mr Brinkman's got it. Phone him and ask. Anyway, I'll be back within forty-eight hours. Now you've got to promise me——'

'Stop fussing! I'll be perfectly all right. Look, if Adam wants you to stay for a few days—er—to have a little holiday or something, then stay. I'll be just fine.'

'I'll be back within forty-eight hours!' Jane reiterated. 'And if you get cheesed off on your own, you'll ask Mrs Graham in, won't you?'

'Yes, yes,' Gerald tutted, finally pushed to impatience. 'Now will you please stop fussing, and get out of here? If you miss that plane, there'll be trouble!' He grinned as he ushered his daughter out of the flat. 'Give Adam my regards!'

'Madam?' The sound of the stewardess's voice brought Jane back to the present. She looked at her blankly.

'I'm sorry, what did you say?'

'Champagne, I asked if you'd like a glass of champagne?'

'No, actually I'd like something stronger,' said Jane. This was one time when she actually felt in need of a drink. 'I'll have a brandy.'

The brandy did nothing to help her calm down. She was irritated at her father's amusement over this whole escapade. She was frantic at the idea of leaving him alone. She was furious at Adam Francis, at the power he had over her. Well, this was the last time he'd use it, of that she was certain! Client or no, as soon as she came face to face with the wretched man, all havoc would break loose!

Barbados time is four hours behind Greenwich Mean Time, so it felt very odd to Jane that despite the long flight it was still only four-thirty in the afternoon when the Captain announced that they were descending into Barbados airport. As far as Jane's body was concerned it was the middle of the evening, and she was already beginning to feel the effects of a frantic morning and the long journey. There was also the tension which had kept her uneasy during the flight, so that sleep had been out of the question. The anger inside her had reached boiling point.

As they circled the land, she gazed out of the window at the splendour of the island sprawling lazily in the Caribbean, at the beautiful white sands, the glorious sunshine and sparkling turquoise sea. It was as if she were entering a different world. But she couldn't allow herself the luxury of enjoying this; the place or even the sight of it. She wanted to be back in London.

Stepping into the heat of the afternoon sun increased Jane's discomfort. She was so inappropriately dressed, still clad in the suit she had worn to the office. A woollen suit, at that! Within twenty minutes she was finished with all the formalities in the airport building. Her passport was stamped. She'd arrived.

No sooner had she wondered what would happen next than a very tall, very thin man came up to her. He was wearing the most ghastly pair of Bermuda shorts, hand-painted in the gaudiest of colours. Jane looked at him in astonishment. While her own clothes were admittedly unsuitable, the informality of his dress was totally alien to her! She could see at once that he was neither West Indian nor European, but she didn't expect to hear him speak to her in a pure American accent.

'Miss Jane Winters?' The man's smile was dazzling. From a very brown face there suddenly appeared a flash of brilliantly white teeth, and the warmth in his eyes brought a friendly response from Jane. She looked down at herself. 'I suppose I wasn't difficult to spot, was I?'

'Well,' he said politely, deliberately missing the point, 'Mr Francis described you to me.' She saw the teeth again. 'I'm Samsam, pleased to welcome you to our glorious islands!' His long, thin fingers encircled her hand fleetingly.

'I'm pleased to meet you—Samsam?' She didn't try to hide her amusement.

'A nickname,' he said cheerily. 'It's a long story, but never mind! Everybody calls me Samsam.' He picked up her overnight case and held out his hand for her briefcase. Jane held on to it. The case contained the legal documents, the reason she was here, the reason for all the inconvenience she'd been put to. She wasn't going to let go of it for a minute.

A short time later she and Samsam were sailing across a calm blue sea, heading for the little island of San Pablo. They were in a white cabin cruiser and Jane was holding her hands at the side of her head in a futile effort to keep her hair in place. Samsam was at the helm, talking non-stop about the Caribbean islands and their attributes.

It wasn't an interest in Samsam's chatter, nor was it the beauty that surrounded her that kept Jane on her feet. It was anger. That and her physical exhaustion had served to make her white-faced. Privately, Samsam wondered whether she was going to be seasick.

'How much farther is it?' Jane spoke loudly in an effort to make herself heard above the wind.

'We're nearly there!' Samsam flashed his teeth at her reassuringly. 'Look ... you can see the island now!'

Jane followed the line of his long, thin arm and there, sure enough, was San Pablo. It was too far away to see clearly; it was shimmering hazily in the low rays of a sinking sun. Jane stared straight ahead of her. A sparkling jewel in a sparkling sea, it looked almost magical, foreign, mysterious and oh, so peaceful.

Samsam was weaving a peculiar path on his approach, explaining that the best part of the island was surrounded by coral reefs. They were approaching from the west. Suddenly he steered sharply towards the south with an expert knowledge of the waters and where their dangers lay. At once they were heading into a small, secluded cove, and as the boat straightened on its course, Jane saw the house.

It was built on two storeys, poised magnificently on the face of a craggy hillside. Contrasted against the immaculate whiteness of the house was the vivid red splash which was a canopy over the entrance. From Jane's vantage point she could see no sign of life and the interior of the house looked black. She shielded her eyes and squinted against the light. In front of the house, on a lower level, she could see the twinkling blue of a swimming pool surrounded by palm trees. And then they were too close to see any more detail.

Alongside the narrow jetty where Samsam moored the boat there was another vessel, a slender, powerful-looking speedboat on the side of which, in black letters, was painted, *Francisco*. She followed Samsam up the stone steps which led to Adam's house, across the paved patio and through the large, sliding glass panels which opened into the living room. There was no one around, and Samsam came to a halt.

It was a huge room, cool and airy. Not only was it cool in the true meaning of the word but the décor, the furniture, everything was geared to give the illusion of coolness. The floor was tiled, the walls were white roughcast plaster; even the furniture was white, very expensive and comfortable-looking. The only real colour in the room came from the paintings, at least half a dozen of them, and from the rugs which were scattered around.

Samsam looked at her apologetically. 'I'm sorry, miss, but Mr Francis must still be in his study. He's spent most of his day in there, making phone calls. I'll take you to him and then I'll put your case in your room.'

One minute later, Jane was face to face with Adam Francis.

'Francisco———' Samsam opened the door of the study and stopped abruptly.

Adam was on the telephone, standing, a cigarette in his free hand. He looked cross. 'I don't want excuses, Hal, I want results. That's what I pay you for, remember?' He spoke sharply into the phone as his eyes came to rest on Jane who was standing, motionless, by Samsam's side. 'Look, Hal, the papers for the Birmingham England site have just arrived. I'll call you back with the details. That'll give you some time to come up with a few more ideas.' Adam put down the phone, his eyes not leaving Jane's for a second.

CHAPTER FIVE

JANE was vaguely aware of Samsam leaving the room, of the door closing behind him, but her eyes stayed on Adam Francis and it was more than she could do to tear them away. It was happening all over again, just as it had seven days ago, in an airport on the other side of the world. The difference was that this time, it was not a feeling of recognition that flooded Jane but a feeling of *inevitability*. For a moment she felt a wild urge to laugh out loud at her own naïvety. How could she ever have doubted that he felt just as attracted to her as she was to him? His face was impassive but it was there, now, in his eyes. Desire. It was crackling between them like electricity, so strong that it seemed almost to have a presence of its own.

The trouble was that, for Jane, it didn't end there. For her, at least, there was much more to it than that. She knew a sudden overwhelming joy at seeing Adam, and that was something quite separate from physical attraction. Her heart was beating so wildly she thought she would pass out. All her anger had melted, so strong were the new emotions aroused by seeing him. Consequently her well-rehearsed attack became drained of all its power. 'You've got a nerve! How dare you bring me all this way to deliver——'

'I know.' Adam held up a hand and sank wearily into his chair. 'I realise I owe you an apology. I've had a—most unusual—week since I left you. I came here yesterday in an effort to escape. This place is supposed to be my retreat. I should never have had a telephone installed . . . I'm sorry, Jane.'

His speech, his apologetic attitude, effectively robbed her of any remaining traces of anger. She stood still, feeling powerless, confused. 'I—well, here are your papers.' She put her briefcase on his desk and he thanked her warmly.

'Come on, you must be exhausted. Let me take you to your room. No doubt Florette will have coffee in the making.'

'Florette?' Her legs seemed to lose all their strength as he put a hand under her elbow and guided her upstairs.

'Samsam's wife. They live in. Florette is just about the best cook on the island, and Samsam is my gardener. He also looks after the place generally for me. I brought him over from Brazil some years ago. He met Florette, who's Jamaican, and—well, they love it here!'

Adam opened the door to a room as bright and airy as the living room downstairs, but Jane didn't take in any of its details, just as she'd barely registered what Adam had been saying. As he opened the French windows on to a balcony, Jane sank into the nearest chair, unable to take her eyes off him. What was happening to her? Why was she reacting so stupidly when she should by now be in the midst of a blazing row?

He turned to face her then, the dappling light of a sinking sun glinting on his dark gold hair, casting shadows on the rugged contours of his face. He spoke her name softly, holding out his hands to her.

Like one who was mesmerised, Jane walked over to him, welcoming the touch, the warm strength of his hands as he took hold of her own. They stood quietly for a moment, each enjoying the sight, the nearness, of the other.

'Adam, I—Why am I here? I accept that you wanted your papers quickly, but why me? Why did I have to be the one——'

He slipped an arm around her shoulders, turning her gently towards the open windows where an endless, glorious sky was visible. A sky that was a myriad colours; orange, gold, lilac, pink. And in the centre of it all was a huge, burning red ball which was the setting sun. Even as they stood, it seemed to sink lower and lower into the dark blue sea. It was breathtakingly beautiful.

'For this,' Adam said softly. 'And for so many other things I want to show you, scenes which will be just as beautiful. I want to show you what life can be like outside that grey, narrow little world you live in.' His arm tightened around her shoulders, and he smiled at the look on her face. 'Also because I want that dinner date you owe me. And, simply, because I like your company.'

'Well, I . . . I suppose that's honest enough.'

'Friends, Jane?'

'Friends? Oh, I see!' She laughed. Adam Francis probably never forgot anything. 'All right. Friends, Adam.'

For Adam, it was a little bit of progress. But he must leave it at that, for the time being. He could feel the tension in her body. She was afraid, trying very hard to fight against the inevitable. Why she was like this, he still had no idea. But his patience with Jane would be infinite. He must put her at her ease.

'Just look at you!' he said then. 'Only you could travel to the Caribbean in a navy-blue business suit geared strictly for the City of London!'

'You didn't give me much option——' Jane tried to protest but his infectious laughter was already getting to her.

'I know, but you gave me quite a scare when you walked into my study, dressed like that, with your official-looking briefcase. I thought you were from the Inland Revenue!'

She giggled at his outrageous lies. 'Okay, if you'll get out of my room, I'll change into the one and only dress I brought with me.'

Adam had already noticed her overnight case. The implications had not escaped him. She was ready to run.

'Fine. I'll have coffee sent up to you now. Then if you'd like to rest for a while, I'll finish my phone calls. See you in the drawing room, later. Shall we say eight-thirty?'

'Eight-thirty.'

Jane closed the door after him and lay down on the bed. As tired as she was, she couldn't possibly sleep. Within minutes she was sitting upright, looking around the room as if there were danger in there. Again, her emotions had been thrown into confusion. Again, she was unable to decide exactly what it was she felt for Adam Francis. But of one thing she was sure: he represented some sort of threat to her. He was far too dangerous for comfort.

Jane had never seen such a vast collection of records and cassettes. Outside a department store, that is. She was flicking through the LPs when Adam joined her in the living room. The moment he came in sight, Jane's breath caught in her throat. He was wearing white moccasins and slacks, with a white shirt which was open half way down his chest. Her heart started hammering again and she was grateful she had something to do with her hands, so he wouldn't notice they were trembling.

'This is some record collection.' She smiled. 'There's something here to suit every taste, I should think.'

'And every mood.' Adam headed for the mirrored bar which was built into a corner of the room, and started filling a cocktail shaker with a carefully measured amount from several bottles. 'Would you like to put something on, Jane? Help yourself.'

'I don't think I'd know how! This hi-fi set looks so complicated, I wouldn't like to touch it before I'd read the instruction manual five or six times! All those buttons . . .'

Adam laughed at her. 'Okay, let me get these cocktails sorted out, then I'll show you how it operates. It's remarkably easy, you know.' He came over to her with a tall, frosted glass that had sugar round the rim and a lot of fruit in it.

Jane looked at it uncertainly. 'What is it?'

'Try it and see—I'll just give you a clue. When in Rome, do as the Romans do.'

'Rum,' she giggled. 'That's what they drink here, isn't it?' She licked her lips appreciatively, much to Adam's amusement. 'Mmm, it's lovely, Adam. What else is in there?'

'That's a trade secret. Don't drink it too fast, though. It's not quite as innocent as it looks.'

Jane didn't heed the warning. She was hungry, she was thirsty and she was very, very nervous. She was also physically exhausted and within minutes the alcohol intensified her sleepiness. 'My father sends his regards, by the way.'

'Thank you.'

'I—er—what time is dinner?'

'Are you hungry?'

'Starving!'

As if on cue, a jovial-looking plump lady came into the room then, and a pair of huge brown eyes swept over Jane in unconcealed curiosity.

'Ah, Florette.' Adam turned to his cook, a mischievous glint in his eye. 'Our guest here is almost faint with hunger. And don't be deceived by her slenderness, Florette. She eats like a horse!'

'Like what?' Florette looked positively alarmed.

'An English expression, dear. Let's just say that Miss Jane will enjoy your food as much as I do.'

'All right, Adam! Thanks very much!' Jane got to her feet and extended her hand. 'You're Samsam's wife, I take it?'

Florette looked a little uncertain, then her eyes danced with laughter, crinkling at the sides as she took Jane's hand in a grip that was remarkably strong. 'Pleased to meet you, Miss Jane.'

'Oh, I'm so sorry,' said Adam. 'I thought you two had met.'

'No. Miss Jane was in the shower when I took coffee to her room.'

'I see. So what time is dinner, then?'

Florette rolled her big brown eyes. 'That's what I came to ask you, Mr Francisco. Only you said I should hold everything because Miss Jane was having a sleep.'

'So I did. Okay, make it as soon as possible.'

Florette bustled out of the room, content with her task. She just loved feeding people who had good appetites.

'Why do they call you Francisco?' Jane sank into the luxurious cushions of the settee.

'That's what I'm known as in Brazil, although it's my middle name, actually. I shortened it to Francis and adopted it as my surname. My real surname is unpronounceable.'

'Really? But your father was American, wasn't he?'

'Yes—of Polish descent. Anyway, Florette stubbornly refuses to drop the "Mr". She thinks it would be too familiar!' He roared with laughter.

Jane didn't think it all that funny. It was a moment before she realised he was laughing because her eyes had closed.

'Am I boring you? Hey, sleepy, is the jet-lag getting to you? You'd better have an early night. We've got a busy sightseeing day ahead of us tomorrow. Didn't you sleep earlier?'

'No, I——' It was a moment before his words penetrated. 'Adam, I'm going home tomorrow! Let's get that clear straight away! I've got responsibilities. I can't hang around here doing nothing.'

Adam thought for a moment before answering. This was certainly not what he had planned. 'Yes, I appreciate that.' In a matter-of-fact voice, he added, 'But I wouldn't advise you to fly tomorrow. Two trips like that in two days will leave you shattered. You wouldn't be fit for work. I know, I've done it.'

It made sense, and Jane certainly didn't relish the thought of another long haul the following day. She was shattered as it was.

'Why don't you go the day after? One day surely won't make much difference, and you mustn't worry about John. I told him to allow a couple of days' travelling time.'

It wasn't Mr Brinkman Jane was worrying about; it was her father. But Adam's reasonableness, and the fact that he didn't expect her to stay longer, persuaded her. One day. Surely just one day wouldn't make much difference to anyone? 'All right. But I'll have to ring Daddy in the morning, and tell him.'

'Agreed,' said Adam. 'I think you're being very wise. And since you will be here, how about seeing the island tomorrow?'

'I might as well.' Jane said it coolly, but the prospect was actually very exciting.

Dinner was served on the patio, the table lit by candlelight, moonlight and the muted lamps dotted around the garden. The evening was perfect, warm and balmy, heady with the sweet scent of the exotic flowers which graced the surrounding gardens. After the superb meal was finished, Jane curled up comfortably on a garden swing and Adam stretched out on a lounger. Florette cleared everything away, delighted in their lavish praise, and brought fresh coffee to them on a tray.

Further down the garden, on a lower level, the reflection of the moon danced on the still water of the swimming pool. Jane glanced up yet again at the huge golden ball hanging in the sky, very low down, as if it were suspended from an invisible string.

'It's hard to believe that's the same moon that shines over London,' she said, almost to herself. 'It's beautiful.'

'Very beautiful,' Adam said softly. But he wasn't looking at the moon. He got up from his chair and sat beside her on the swing. 'No, don't move,' he said quietly. 'I've been wanting to do this since you arrived.' He reached out and took off the slide which was holding her hair in place at the nape. 'I must say that seeing you with your hair released from that awful bun was some improvement, but this . . .' He ran his fingers through the length of her hair, letting it fall below her shoulders. 'That's better. You have such beautiful hair, Jane. Don't ever tie it up again.'

It seemed that Jane's breathing stopped in those

brief moments as he sat very close to her, his intense green eyes travelling over her face and its frame of silken dark brown hair. The faint scent of his aftershave, the size and the very power of him, so near to her, combined to make her feel heady. Her pulses were throbbing and everything in her cried out for his kiss—and feared it at the same time. But fear was the stronger emotion, and she stiffened, edging away from him.

Adam wanted to kiss her, to take her in his arms and make love to her there and then. It was all he could manage to move away from her. But he had seen the fear, again, in her beautiful tawny-gold eyes. For the moment, those eyes were the only means he had of learning about her.

'Did young Meekins mention that I'd asked him to find me a house in London? A house or a flat—something I can rent for about six months?' He watched Jane's response carefully. Even this seemed to alarm her.

'No—I—what did you do that for?'

'I've got a lot to do on the British side of things. I shall oversee the start of the Birmingham project, for one thing. That's why I've been so busy this past week. I've been delegating. I'm trying to disengage myself from my American work so I can be free to spend the next six months in your fair country.'

'I see.' Jane's heart sank. So Adam was going to be on the scene for the next six months. She was flummoxed, wondering how she would be able to avoid him.

'Yes, I thought Meekins would have mentioned it to you when he took you out last week. You know, on the evening you should have been with me.'

'We didn't go out,' Jane said hastily. 'Paul spent that evening in Birmingham. He didn't want to risk being late for the auction.'

'Wise of him,' Adam said wryly. 'I shouldn't have been at all pleased if he'd done that. So did you see him later in the week?'

Jane shifted her position and the swing moved gently backwards and forwards. 'No. You—you've got it all wrong about me and Paul, you know. There's nothing in it.' She had to put an end to this. She'd satisfied herself that Paul and Adam had not discussed her, but there was still the possibility that they might . . . Of course, it was all her own fault she was in this mess in the first place.

Adam was watching her closely. 'Jane, who is it that hurt you so deeply?'

The question came like a bolt out of the blue, and Jane's head came up with a snap. 'What are you talking about?'

'I've told you before, your defences are up against men in general. You're positively afraid of me—and I'm only a friend! You're terrified of any kind of involvement. And it's all because someone hurt you in the past.'

'You're wrong! There wasn't—there never was—anyone! I don't understand you, any of this! You're always asking me questions, Adam. Why don't you just leave me alone?'

She got to her feet, but Adam was beside her in a flash, his retaining hand on her shoulder. 'Sit down and finish your coffee. You can't run away from me, Jane. You cannot and you may not. We're friends, aren't we? I won't ask any more questions, if that's what you want.'

She looked up at him uncertainly, trembling beneath his touch. 'It's true that I don't want any involvement. Is that perfectly clear? And my reasons are my own.'

'Very well.' He sighed. 'Ah, Jane, you're always making things clear to me! You're an incredibly

beautiful girl, and the clearest thing to me is that one
day a man will come into your life who'll love you so
much that he won't be deterred by all your barriers.
He'll love you so much that he'll want to help you
overcome them. And when that is achieved, he'll ask
you to marry him. Having got so far, of course, he
won't take no for an answer . . . Did you ever consider
that this might happen?'

'I've never heard such romantic tripe in all my life!'
She stepped sharply away from him, trembling from
head to foot.

'You know, that's what's lacking in your life—
romance.'

She spun round on him angrily, an unaccountable
rush of tears stinging her eyes. 'Life isn't romantic!
Life is cruel and unfair! Where have you been all your
life? You should have learnt that for yourself by now!
I will never marry! I just wish you wouldn't talk such
rubbish to me!'

'Never, Jane?'

'*Never!*'

'All right,' he shrugged, 'there's no need to get so
uptight about a purely hypothetical conversation.'

Jane sank wearily on to the swing. Adam's eyes were
sparkling with amusement. He was mocking her.
Again. Oh, why did he persist in teasing her so? 'If
you want my company, just keep to general topics, will
you? Otherwise I'll——'

'I'll do better than that,' Adam smiled. 'I'll try to
figure out how the hi-fi works, and then we can have
some music. Nothing too romantic, of course.'

Jane threw him a filthy look, but inwardly she felt
much more relaxed. She felt she'd cleared up quite a
few things. She'd put him in his place, and about time,
too. He was too familiar, too nosey, and far, far too
attractive. She didn't worry about his attractiveness,
though, not any more. She was fully in control of the

situation now. And with only one more day in his company, there really was nothing to be afraid of . . .

When Adam came back she was sound asleep.

He smiled, put down the two glasses of brandy he had brought and stood, just watching her. In sleep she looked so incredibly vulnerable that his heart twisted painfully. Some son of a bitch had hurt her very badly indeed. He had considered several possibilities which would explain Jane's behaviour, but this had been his main theory. He wondered how long it had been since it happened. But that didn't really matter. What mattered was that she was still carrying the scars. She was afraid to trust to the extent that she wouldn't even admit to him he had been right in his assumption. But her anger had told him, her anger and the words she had used.

Very gently he lifted her into his arms and carried her to her bed. It required no effort at all. She felt light and fragile as he cradled her against him. He laid her down, feeling an overwhelming sense of protectiveness, vowing that he would make everything right again for her. He would show her she need never again be afraid; of him, or of anything else in the world. He would erase those scars, and it wouldn't be long before he did it. What had happened between them was so strong, so powerful that she, even she, would not be able to fight it for much longer.

As he looked down at her, her silken hair spread wildly against the pillows, desire for her momentarily blotted out all his rational thinking. He wanted her as he had never wanted any other woman in his life. His pulses were throbbing, the blood coursing through his veins. He moved away from the bed, his hands clenching into fists as sanity returned. Not yet. Not yet. If he touched her now, he wouldn't be able to stop.

CHAPTER SIX

THE sun was streaming through the windows, the sky was a perfect azure and the palm trees rustled very gently in the light breeze. Never before had Jane seen so much natural colour, the sea, the sky, the sun, the greenery, the profusion of flowers in the grounds below her. The beach was sparkling in its whiteness, even the very earth looked richer and more colourful.

She stepped back inside her room, filled with a sense of wellbeing. She even knew a temporary peace. From her bedroom extension she had just telephoned her father. He was all right, having what he called one of his good days. Tomorrow she would be with him, but for the moment there was this glorious day, and she intended to enjoy it. There had been a residue of guilt inside her at the idea of having this day in a paradise on the other side of the world. But Gerald had erased that. Stay, he'd said, stay for as long as you like. It was so silly of him—as if she could!

She poured herself a second cup of tea and pondered over the most immediate problem. What to wear. If Florette had thought it peculiar to find Jane waking up in bed fully clothed, she had said nothing. She had just put down the tea tray, opened the windows and laughingly informed Jane she had a big breakfast under way.

Sitting in her underwear, Jane looked over at her discarded dress. It was linen, pink. It would have done for today. But after sleeping in it, it was unfit to be worn. Suddenly she was laughing. Adam had deposited her on her bed without even removing her dress. He'd probably been piqued because she had firmly put him in his place, then proceeded to fall asleep on him!

What on earth had she worried about? She could handle Adam Francis almost as easily as she handled the Paul Meekins of this world. Almost. He had left her fully clothed. He had never even attempted to kiss her. Come to think of it, he hadn't actually done anything to make her so wary, so distrustful. On that very satisfactory note she drained her cup and padded into the bathroom.

The first half of the day was active, if not hectic. Adam tried his best to show Jane all the sights. They set off in a pale blue, open-topped sports car, armed with a picnic basket and a cold box in which there was enough food for six, and made their first stop at a bustling market in the village centre. That in itself was an excursion. Jane had flatly refused Adam's offer of buying her clothes in the fashionable part of the island and had insisted he take her somewhere she could pick up a few things cheaply. They shared a great deal of laughter at the puzzled faces of the indigenous people as Jane flitted from stall to stall in a navy-blue woollen suit which looked, and was, utterly ridiculous on San Pablo.

On a dress, sandals, shorts, a halter-neck top and a bikini she spent some of her own money and all that Mr Brinkman had given her—not at all what he'd intended his petty cash to be spent on! In another fit of laughter they drove off to see the sights, the sugar-cane fields, the cocoa and nutmeg crops, the banana plantations, and Adam kept up a fascinating, running commentary.

They picnicked on a beach on the far side of the island. It didn't afford them the solitude Adam's private beach would have, but it was fun just to sit and watch the people of various sizes, colours and shapes sunning themselves or splashing about in the water.

Jane stretched out contentedly, her perfect, slender figure attracting the attention of every male passer-by, regardless of his age. She'd changed in a little cabin behind one of the market stalls, and the halter-neck top and tight white shorts left little to the imagination.

Adam finished the last of their wine and gave her a gentle nudge. 'Are you falling asleep on me again?'

'Yes and no.'

'We could take the boat out and go fishing later, if that appeals to you. Does it? And please don't say yes and no!'

'Fishing?' She opened her eyes and pulled a face at him. 'No. There,' she giggled, 'is that positive enough for you? Fishing is not for me. My father's the fisherman in the family. At least, he was before . . .' Her voice trailed off.

'What kind of fishing? Sea fishing?'

'Any kind!' Jane laughed then, as happy memories flashed through her mind. She could hear her mother telling Gerald not to get too wet, to remember to eat his packed lunch, to throw back his catch and not be tempted to bring the 'poor creatures' home for supper. Every weekend it would be the same, Moira teasing her husband and him loving every minute of it.

'Really?' Adam said keenly. 'Well, we have a superb lake here on the island and of course there's a whole sea full of fish out there . . . Jane, what do you and Gerald normally do at Christmas?'

It was such a swift change of subject that she looked at him in confusion.

'I mean, do you normally visit relatives, or have relatives over to your place? Or what?'

'No. The—the only relatives we have left are Mother's family, and they're still in Scotland. We get on very well, but we hardly see them. Why?'

'I was thinking. Christmas is only a couple of

months away. How about you and Gerald coming out here for a holiday?'

Jane stared at him, not realising she was doing so. A dozen thoughts and emotions were suddenly jumbled inside her. There was sadness because the idea was out of the question, and pain at the reason for that. Gerald could never make the journey. Oh, but he would so love it here . . . Apart from all this Jane knew a rush of gratitude towards Adam for extending the invitation. How very, very kind of him! It seemed that his kindness to Gerald on the night of their meeting had been genuine—the way he had talked engineering with him, the way he had listened intently while Gerald went on at length about the wife he had lost. Adam Francis, Adam Francis was really——

'Jane?'

'Yes. I—I was just thinking about it. But I'm afraid the answer is no. Thank you. It was a very kind thought, Adam.'

'Can you give me a reason?'

She shook her head and looked away from him. He didn't push it; he'd invite them again. He just said, 'Well, check with Gerald before you finally decide. I mean, you shouldn't answer on his behalf.'

'All right.' She would have said almost anything in order to drop the subject. There was a pain inside her the like of which she'd never known before. 'Shall we go? I'd like to take a siesta since you've got a packed programme for me this evening.' Adam had told her he had a treat in store, but she had no idea what it was.

For Jane, the day lost some of its magic after that. She had come down to earth with a bang. She wasn't a different person in a different world. She was Jane Winters, and she had been foolish enough to let her guard drop. But the conversation on the beach had put it firmly back in place again—and this time it would stay there.

Outwardly she remained lighthearted. Adam had been kindness itself and she didn't want to spoil anything for him. He'd been such a perfect, charming host. When they got back to his house and he suggested a swim, Jane went along with the idea. Sleep would be out of the question now, anyway. The pain that had settled inside her was still there, though she couldn't pinpoint the cause of it. Probably she was worrying about Gerald; the conversation on the beach had brought him to the forefront of her mind.

Jane took hold of the rails and started to pull herself out of the water, narrowly escaping Adam as he tried to prevent her.

'Hey! I challenged you to race *twice* round the pool,' he protested. 'Do you concede defeat?'

She swished the hair from her face and laughed at him, making a determined effort to keep in the mood of things. 'No! Certainly not! You couldn't have beaten me, so I'm letting you off.'

'Crazy woman!'

They flopped down on the mattresses at the side of the swimming pool, Jane positioning herself so the top half of her body was under the shade of a palm tree. She couldn't have survived the afternoon sun without having a swim and her pale skin was too delicate to take much exposure. Adam was lying close to her, his eyes closed and his hand resting lightly on her arm.

Jane's eyes moved slowly along the length of his body, the strong, muscled legs, the narrow hips and the very tight, very brief trunks that were clinging there, their whiteness making a stark contrast against his deeply tanned skin. His chest was magnificent, broad and deep and strong, covered in a mass of fair hair which was still wet from his swim.

Jane drank in the sight of him, for the moment forgetting all her problems, all her worries. Adam

Francis had the body of an athlete and a ruggedly attractive face that would make even the most casual passer-by turn around for a second look. Just looking at him like this made her pulses pound, her heart beat faster. He simply oozed masculinity, strength, virility ... She didn't even know what she'd done until it was too late. Like a pin to a magnet she was drawn to him. As if by a will of its own, her hand reached out to caress his chest, his shoulders. His eyes came open instantly, the expression in them changing, unreadable, until they darkened with an unmistakable emotion.

And then he was kissing her, kissing her as she'd never been kissed before. There was an instant eruption, an explosion of the desire that had been slowly mounting in both of them. She returned his kiss, his increasingly intimate caresses, forgetting who she was and where she was, knowing only that she had longed for this.

This was the inevitable.

It was also the impossible.

Suddenly she was being lifted and the world receded, returned, weaved around her as she fought for control. Impossible, impossible! She struggled to get her feet to the ground, but Adam held onto her tightly.

'Adam, no! Please. *Please!*' She pushed frantically against his chest, seeing his frown, the confusion in his eyes.

'Hush, darling, it's all right. I'm taking you to my room.' He lowered his cheek to hers, nuzzling against her, planting little kisses on her throat. 'We won't be disturbed, my darling. There's nobody in the——'

'No!' she screamed. Dear heaven, did he not understand what she was saying? 'Put me down, Adam. Put me down!'

He put her down, still holding her tightly against

him, his breathing ragged, his hands shaking as he held her close. 'Jane,' he said softly, his voice thick with desire, 'don't ever—don't you realise——' He stopped short at what he saw in her eyes. Stark fear. From the depths of his being a moan escaped from him and he cradled her head against his shoulder.

'Adam, I didn't mean . . . I didn't want this——'

'You started it, Jane.'

'I know, and I'm sorry, but I . . . I don't want——'

'I know. You don't want any involvement. Yet your body tells me otherwise.'

'I thought we were just friends,' she said stupidly.

His laugh was short, his smile wry. 'Friends—lovers. Isn't that a natural progression? Sooner or later we're going to make love. You know that as well as I do.'

'No!' She pulled away from him sharply, turning her back, unable to face him. 'It isn't going to be that way! That's *not* what I want!'

It was a long moment before he answered her. Adam Francis was not a cool-blooded Englishman, nor did he share Jane's lack of experience. He wanted her, and it was not easy to switch off like this. Making love was the most natural thing in the world to him. But he was thinking of the fear he had seen in her eyes. Had it been merely the fear of a young and inexperienced woman he could easily have overcome it, and led her gently and tenderly into the delights of the sensual she had not yet tasted. Soon he would do that. He would make her his own once and for ever. But for the moment he must leave her alone. He didn't just want her body. He wanted her acquiescence, her mind, her *heart*.

He sighed deeply, silently. In a way, he already had her heart. She had fallen in love with him on the evening they met, but she was fighting against it with everything in her, trying constantly, one way or another, to run from him. Until she admitted what had happened, firstly to herself, he could not tell her how he felt. To do that would be to risk frightening her away from him completely.

'All right, Jane,' he said softly. 'If it isn't what you want, then so be it.'

Relief flooded through Jane as she turned to face him. He was smiling at her patiently, his clear green eyes telling her everything was all right again. This had all been her fault, she knew that, and she wasn't proud of herself. In fact she was growing increasingly embarrassed at the way she had lost control, led him on . . .

'I—I think I'll take a nap now, Adam. If you'll excuse me——'

'Oh, no you don't!' He grinned at her, not prepared to allow any kind of strain to develop between them. 'You're not going to run away from me. Go into the kitchen and make a pot of tea. Bring it on to the patio and we'll watch the sun go down.'

'Tea?' she said blankly, completely distracted from her embarrassment. 'I shouldn't have thought you'd be the——'

'The afternoon tea type? I'm not. Any more than I'm the Ovaltine type! I'll be having something stronger. The tea's for you. I . . .' He smiled, that slow, audacious smile which made his eyes sparkle. Jane was laughing before he even finished what he was saying, knowing he was about to tease her mercilessly. 'I always keep a supply of tea here—just in case any cool and ever-so-proper Englishwomen drop in on me.'

'Adam!' She gave him a playful dig in the ribs. How come he always managed to make her laugh, in spite of herself?

'Tell me, Jane, is that why the English are always drinking tea—in the hope that it'll melt their reserve?'

Jane was feeling mellow, content, replete—and a little tipsy. It seemed that the magic of the island was getting to her all over again. The surprise Adam had had in store for her was every bit as good as he had promised it would be. They were sitting at a floorside table in an open air night-club under a star-studded sky. It was a small place, intimate and very romantic, set against a background of palmtrees lit up with fairy lights.

Jane had heard of places such as this, but she had never imagined she would have the chance to see one. Set at the foot of the stage, in a semi-circle, were dozens of earthenware pots overflowing with brightly coloured flowers. Several couples were on the dance floor, swaying dreamily to the sentimental music created by a combo on the stage. The atmosphere was so relaxed, so romantic; everyone was casually but nicely dressed, and the worry Jane had had over her own attire had been dispelled. She was wearing the simple white dress she had bought in the market that morning. It was cotton, sleeveless, with a low neck and thin shoulder-straps. It fitted her perfectly at the waist and flared out a little in the skirt and it was, it seemed, just the right thing.

Adam was wearing dark blue slacks and shirt—with no tie. But of course, that would have been against his principles! He had come in wearing a jacket, and had discarded it within ten minutes.

Jane pushed her plate away and sat back, sighing contentedly. 'Adam, that was the most delicious meal I've ever had—even if I didn't recognise half the contents of the salad!'

'Bounties of the island,' he smiled.

'And the sauce? What was in the sauce that came with the steak?'

'Brandy. You'd better watch it. Two sundowners, three glasses of wine and brandy sauce. Do you think you ought, Jane?'

She picked up her empty wineglass and peered at him over the top of it, giggling. 'Someone once told me that in life I should try everything once and some things twice.'

'Not I,' he said, as if the very idea were shocking. He refilled her glass, then curled his hand around the slender bones of her wrist. 'And you must realise that the man who told you that was not referring to drinks.'

She flushed, looking more beautiful than she could ever know. 'Who says it was a man?'

'I do. Because that's a seduction line if ever I heard one!'

Jane suppressed her smile, realising that it was she, now, who was doing the flirting. Why was it Adam had such a peculiar effect on her? He brought out in her sides of her own nature she didn't know existed. With him she laughed, she blushed, she got angry. One way or another, she never managed to maintain her cool veneer. She liked him so much, so very much.

She turned her hand slightly, so that it was enveloped by his own. 'Adam, I'm having such a lovely time. Thank you for bringing me here. Thank you for everything. It's been so nice.'

'Hey, don't make it sound so final! You're not really going to desert me tomorrow, are you? Stay on for a while, Jane. Just a few more days.'

'I can't.' She tried to pull her hand away, but Adam held on to it tightly.

'Of course you can. I'll fix it with John, don't worry about that.'

'No. No, I—I have to go back tomorrow.' There was such a finality about her voice that he decided not to pursue the matter just then. Later, he would persuade her. He was sure of it.

Suddenly all the lights in the club went off. 'What is it?' Jane was slightly alarmed. 'A power cut?'

She could still see Adam from the soft glow of the candlelight. He laughed quietly. 'No. Just time for a change of mood. You haven't seen anything yet. It might seem late to you, but in the Caribbean the night is young. The show's only just starting.'

And so it was. When the lights came on again there was a steel band on stage and the atmosphere changed completely as their lively, calypso music filled the air, bringing onto the dancefloor the more adventurous.

'Come on!' Adam tugged at Jane's hand.

'I can't dance to this!'

He looked heavenward. 'Don't be so stuffy, Miss Winters. Just do your own thing.'

Jane hadn't enjoyed herself so much since—well, she couldn't remember when. Actually, she'd never had such a wonderful time. They danced and they danced, separately, as everyone else was doing, until the lights went off again and the dance floor was cleared to make way for the limbo dancers.

They went back to their table and Adam ordered coffee. Jane clapped her hands together in excitement as the announcement was made about the limbo dancers, and the show began. The place was throbbing with the beat of drums, throbbing with an excitement which seemed to get inside Jane's blood. At midnight, the Voodoo dancers came on and the excitement heightened even further. She watched the performance in total fascination, almost hypnotised by their painted faces, their colourful, strange costumes and the beat, beat, beat of the drums as they played faster and faster.

Adam was watching Jane, enchanted by her enchantment at all she was seeing. She thought herself sophisticated, when she was actually a babe as far as worldly matters were concerned; she thought herself tough, when she was really afraid. Of what, he didn't know. She was still very much a mystery to him. He wanted to show her what life could be like when she allowed herself to relax and be happy—like now.

When the show finished, the mood reverted to one of romantic relaxation. The combo came on stage and resumed their soft music. Several couples left, but those who stayed on into the early hours of the morning made their way on to the dance floor, caught up in the sheer magic of the evening.

'Okay, let's join the dancers.' Jane laughed softly. 'This is much more my style.'

'Darling, it'll be my pleasure.' Adam was already on his feet.

They didn't dance for long. Adam pulled her close, enfolding her in his arms, holding her firmly but gently against him as they swayed to the music. Desire ripped through Jane like a forest fire. She leaned her head against his shoulder, intoxicated by the clean, masculine smell of him, the warm strength of his body touching hers.

She felt as if she were floating on air. For her, they were the only couple on the floor, the only couple in the world. Her arms came up and she laced her fingers into the crispness of his hair, the softness of her body pressing closer and closer to his. Adam's lips were against her temple, his hands low down on the curve of her hips. His response was as immediate as hers, his breathing quickening as the seconds passed.

His hands slid upwards, encircling her waist, and he moved her gently away from him, allowing a little distance to separate their bodies. 'It's no use, Jane.' His voice was low, husky, his lips close to her ear. 'We'd better get off this dance floor—and fast! I'm finding it increasingly difficult to conceal my feelings for you.'

Jane blushed to the roots of her hair as he guided her from the floor. By unspoken agreement they didn't linger at their table. Adam pocketed his cigarettes,

Jane picked up her bag, and they left. She was trembling from head to foot. They were going home to make love. He knew it, she knew it, and a handful of other people knew it, too.

She shivered as he opened the car door for her. Adam slipped his jacket around her shoulders, turning her around to face him. His lips came down on hers hungrily, passionately, and Jane's lips parted beneath his, allowing, inviting, welcoming the erotic exploration of his mouth.

On a low moan, Adam pulled away from her, muttering something in a foreign language. He sat behind the wheel for a moment, his big hands gripping the steering wheel tightly before he made any move to start the car. They were silent, communicating as they never had before. They were on the far side of the island, and they wanted each other *now*. Jane looked away from him, her heartbeat pounding in her ears as she held her hands tightly together in an effort to stop them trembling.

He fired the engine and they moved off into the starry darkness of the night.

They drove in silence, Jane's hair billowing wildly in the open-topped car. Beneath lowered lashes she watched him, imagining his long, strong fingers on her body, longing to feel again the touch of his lips on hers. It was as if she were floating along in a dream. She knew, now, that it wasn't the island that held magic for her—it was Adam. How she wanted him, how she loved him——

The sudden realisation, the shock of it, hit her like a body blow. Her mind reeled. Panic overruled all her other emotions. Dear heaven, she loved him! This was never supposed to happen. Never! Not with him, not with anyone. All this time, she had protected herself . . . she had given her feelings for Adam so many different labels until, now, she was forced to give them the right name. Respect, admiration, friendship, excitement, desire ... *She'd fallen in love with him.*

She went rigid.

Adam eased the car slowly on to the driveway at the back of the house. Samsam's quarters were there, and they entered the house quietly. Adam reached for Jane as soon as they got into the living room, but she wrenched herself away from him almost violently, her voice catching on a sob. 'I'm sorry, Adam. Oh, Adam, I'm so very sorry. I—I can't ...'

In the next few moments everything seemed to happen in slow motion. She felt the bite of his fingers on her arms, saw the look of fury in his eyes. It went as quickly as it came—but it was something she hoped never to see again. She felt desolate, utterly, utterly desolate. She loved Adam, but she loved her father, too. And Gerald came first. He always had and he always would. He needed her, and Jane would allow nobody—*but nobody*—to come between herself and her father's needs. As things stood, now, she would get over Adam Francis, given time. But if she made love with him, not only would he know her feelings for him—she would also be lost. It would be that much harder to get over——

Suddenly she was crushed against him, then his hands were stroking her hair gently, ever so gently. It wasn't until she tasted the salt tears on her lips that she realised she was crying.

'Oh, no, don't cry, Jane. Please don't cry. I can't bear it!' Adam eased her into a chair. Whatever it was that haunted this girl, he could handle. But he couldn't bear to see her looking so incredibly unhappy.

'We've got to talk.' He pressed a large glass of brandy into her hands and sat down facing her. 'What is this battle that rages inside you? Why are you such a crazy, mixed-up kid?'

'I'm not,' she said quietly. For her, the crisis had passed. She felt cold inside—cold, but very calm. She knew what she had to do. 'We're different, that's all. It's different for you, Adam. I can't just reach out and take my pleasures without thought of——'

'I'm not talking about sex, Jane. I'm talking about us. I was right about your being hurt in the past, wasn't I? Is that why you don't trust me?'

'It isn't that I don't trust you. You—oh, you don't understand!'

'I'm trying to.' Adam was grave, his eyes pleading with her. 'How can I understand you when you won't tell me anything? What is it that haunts you, Jane? Tell me. I can help you. There's nothing we can't handle. *Nothing*.'

In reply, Jane got stiffly to her feet. When she spoke, her voice was as cold as ice. 'Nothing can come of this, Adam. I'm taking the first available flight out of here tomorrow. Thank you ... for everything.'

He stared at her in amazement as she walked away. He didn't go after her; he knew it would be hopeless. He got up, took a bottle of Scotch from the bar and stretched out on the settee.

It was time for a rethink.

CHAPTER SEVEN

SHE was already sitting on the patio when Adam came down the next day. She was wearing her suit, her overnight case and her briefcase were by her side. Obviously, neither Samsam nor Florette had mentioned the news to her.

Adam was joyous. Fate was on his side. But of

course it was; Jane Winters was meant for him, and Fate was lending a helping hand.

Jane started as he came into view. He was wearing a bath towel, his hair still wet from his shower. 'Good morning.' She smiled distantly, though her heart contracted painfully at the sight of him.

'Good morning, Jane.' He waved the morning newspaper at her. 'I have good news for you. You can't go home today.'

'Good—what are you talking about?'

'It's good news because it relieves you of any responsibility, doesn't it?' He grinned. 'I mean, it's something beyond your control, so nobody can blame you, and you can't blame yourself. I'll phone John Brinkman and explain things for you.'

She was on her feet. 'What are you talking about?'

Adam handed her the paper. 'There's been a lightning strike. The control tower staff, all the ground staff at the Caribbean airports.'

Jane gasped, scanning the paper. 'I can't see anything.'

'Apparently it was on the radio last night. Samsam's just told me. It's there—in the Stop Press.'

So it was.

Appalled, panic-stricken, she sank back into her chair, only to jump up again immediately. 'I must phone Daddy at once.'

Adam's brows rose in surprise. 'Yes, of course. Though I thought you'd have been more concerned about John. Phone him, too. Or would you rather I did it?'

'The heck with work,' she said without thinking. 'It's my——' Adam was laughing, and she got furious with him. 'You needn't look so smug about this, Adam!'

'The heck with work,' he repeated. 'Quite right, too. Why don't you just relax and resign yourself to a few days' holiday?'

'A few days?' The idea made the colour fade from her face. 'You don't think it'll come to that, do you?'

He was laughing like a drain. 'You don't think strikes are peculiar to England?'

Jane didn't even bother to answer that. There had to be some way out of this. 'Look, Adam, you've got influence. There must be some way you can get me out of here.'

The laughter died from his face. She was reacting very strangely. He didn't want to help her on her way, didn't understand why she was so upset. 'Without the control tower, nothing flies. Nothing.'

'Then you can at least make a few phone calls and try to get more details, see how long this nonsense is going to last.' She slapped her hand against the newspaper. 'It says nothing in here!'

'That's my girl! As stubborn as the day is long, aren't you?'

'Yes,' she said icily, knowing full well what he was getting at. She would tell him nothing. 'Please, Adam. Suffice it to say that this is important to me.'

'Very well.' Adam got lazily to his feet. 'I'll see what I can find out.' But he didn't go indoors. Instead, he reached out to touch her face, his fingers holding her chin firmly, forcing her to look into his eyes. 'But don't think for one minute you're fooling me. You won't be surprised to learn that I couldn't sleep last night. Any more than you could, probably. I did a great deal of thinking. You've been trying to run away from me since the moment we met. Well, you can't— I've told you that before. You're desperate to get off this island because you've fallen in love with me—and last night you finally realised it. And for some obscure reason, the knowledge terrifies you.'

Jane felt as if her legs would give way beneath her. Dear heaven, he was so perceptive ... too perceptive for his own good. She couldn't speak. She was casting about frantically for a retort, a denial which would be feasible. 'You're incurably romantic, Adam,' she said coldly. 'Stupidly so. I've told you before not to talk such romantic rubbish to me. You should try explaining your own behaviour instead of analysing mine. You brought me out here for one thing, and one thing only. You've staged the most elaborate seduction scene imaginable—and you're mad because it all went wrong.'

She saw his eyes close, felt his fingers tighten on the bones of her chin. Then he let go of her. 'You can't insult me like that, Jane. You know what happened to us at London airport. I'm going to get to the bottom of this, I warn you now.'

Inwardly, she was weeping. Weeping for what couldn't be. She had to stop this thing from going any further, she just had to. Her insults hadn't worked, but there was still her good old standby—the non-existent boy-friend. It had worked with Paul Meekins and there was no reason why it shouldn't work with Adam. Furthermore, she could tell Adam with a great deal of conviction because, in a way, she'd be telling him the truth. She lifted her head proudly. 'You flatter yourself, Adam. You're being very blind and very stupid. All right, since you're determined to know what it is with me, I'll tell you. You mean nothing to me emotionally. You've been fixed with the idea that I want to run away from you. Why don't you ask yourself instead why I'm eager to get home? There's someone else. There's someone in London whom I love very deeply. It's him I want to get back to. He's the reason I couldn't give myself to you in a fit of passion—meaningless passion. He's the reason I don't want any involvement. Don't you see? I'm already involved!'

Conviction or no, it didn't work.

'Try again,' he said. 'You can do better than that.'

Adam went into his study. She was lying in her teeth, and he'd been in danger of losing his temper with her. He slammed his fist against the desk, the question still paramount in his mind: why was she like this? Why was she lying? He had one answer, one piece of the puzzle that was Jane, but it wasn't enough. Not now. The more he learned about her, the more he realised there was more to this thing than a bad emotional experience in her past. Without the rest of the picture, he had no way of knowing where this piece of information fitted in. He had never known such frustration. Actually, it was there, the rest of the picture, taunting him from somewhere in the back of his mind. But he just couldn't put it together. At that moment he was too angry to think straight.

He made his phone call and discovered that the strike was expected to last for three days. That would take him to the end of the week, then he would have to go back to New York. Still, a lot could happen in three days.

For Jane, those remaining days with Adam were the strangest days of her life. From the privacy of her bedroom she telephoned her father each morning and evening. She was desperate with worry, her nerves growing more and more taut as time ticked by. Despite what Gerald told her, she knew he was going through a bad patch. The tiredness in his voice was unmistakable, belying his assurances that he was fine, just fine.

And there was Adam. Loving him made her so vulnerable, leaving her wide open for the hurt she had vowed no man would ever again be capable of inflicting upon her. But he remained as natural and as easygoing as ever. He made no attempt to make love to her, but he refused to let her be alone. He went with her when she walked on the beach, he took her out to lunch, he took her shopping in the fashionable part of the island, insisting on buying her far more than she needed for the rest of her stay.

It seemed to Jane that the more she was with Adam, the less she knew herself. His presence became less of a threat and more of . . . well, almost a comfort to her. He encouraged her to talk about general things, and he told her a great deal about himself, his childhood in Brazil, the way he had started his business.

It was strange. It was as if something were happening inside Jane over which she had no control. She didn't like what was happening, nor could she identify it, but it seemed she was powerless to resist it.

She left San Pablo on the Saturday morning. Over breakfast, Adam told her there was a seat reserved for her on the afternoon flight.

'So with the time difference, I'll get home about—what?'

'In the middle of the night, I'm afraid.' He waited, knowing what would come next.

'I must ring Daddy and let him know.' She got to her feet, but Adam caught hold of her hand.

'Sit down, Jane. I want to talk to you. I'll ring Gerald later, tell him you're on your way.'

'No! I mean, it's okay, I—I'll do it. Go on, Adam, what is it you want to say?'

If Adam had needed any further confirmation that he was right, Jane's reaction had just given it to him. Over the past three days the rest of the picture had drawn itself for him. Because it was the last thing on earth he had expected, he had been blind to it at first. But by observing her, searching his memory and bearing in mind what he had known about Jane from the start, he was in no doubt at all that he had reached the right conclusion. He was prepared for what was to come, and he wanted to cushion Jane as much as possible—but it was very important that the words came from her own lips.

'Jane, I thought you'd lied to me a few days ago, when you told me there was already someone with whom you were involved. Then I watched you grow increasingly anxious, and the look in your eyes changed from that of the frightened to that of the haunted. No matter what I tried to distract you, your anxiety only increased. Tell me about it, Jane. Tell me now why you and Gerald can't come here for Christmas.'

Jane put down her coffee cup, meeting the steady gaze of clear, green eyes. Wise eyes. Loving eyes. Sad eyes. He'd guessed, there was no doubt.

'You have to say it, Jane.' Adam took hold of her hands, holding them tightly, as if he would pour into her some of his own strength. Just as he had been trying to for the past couple of days.

'I—It's . . . a degenerative disease of the bones. There's nothing we . . . The prognosis . . .'

Adam could feel the skin on his face growing tighter, colder. 'How bad is . . . how long?'

'Three years, five maybe. I don't know. Even the doctors don't know how——' She tried to pull her hands away from his, but Adam would not allow her to break their connection. He squeezed gently, his voice very, very quiet. 'Well done, Jane. Thank you . . . for trusting me at last.'

She didn't utter a sound. She just blinked. He thought she would cry; in a way he hoped she would, but there were no tears, no words.

'I love you, Jane—you know that already. I want you to remember this when you leave me today. I love you more than anything in the world. And there's nothing we can't handle—*together*. Together, Jane. That's how it's going to be from now on. I'll be in London next weekend, and from then on we'll never——'

'No.'

For a split second, Adam felt an emotion which was totally alien to him. It was caused by the tone of her voice, so lifeless, so final. But what was there to fear now? She would come round, it was only a matter of time. He thought of Gerald, and the meaning of the phrase suddenly turned sour.

Poor Gerald.

'Francisco?' Samsam stepped on to the patio, looking uncertainly from one to the other. 'We ought to be leaving soon.'

'Ten minutes, Samsam.' He let go of Jane's hands. 'Go and make your phone call, darling.'

The need for privacy gone, Jane phoned her father from the study. She had already packed, and Adam was waiting for her on the patio. He held his arms open and she walked straight into them, because she couldn't stop herself from doing so. Just once more, she wanted to feel the strength of his arms around her. He told her again how he loved her, and with a kiss unlike any other kiss he'd given her, he told her yet again.

She bade him goodbye in a voice which was barely audible. He loved her, he'd said. From next week onwards they would always be together, he'd said. But Jane Winters did not believe in daydreams.

From the jetty she turned to look up at him. She returned his wave, and suddenly she was plunged back into the past. As she waved goodbye to Adam, it was Billy she was thinking of.

Adam stood on the patio a long time after the boat had disappeared from view. His hands were thrust deeply into his trouser pockets. He could feel the sun beating on his back, doing nothing to warm him. For the first time in many years he was thinking about his own mortality. He had made a promise to himself which he couldn't fulfil. He could not make everything in Jane's world right again.

Nobody could.

He sighed deeply, a great, shuddering sigh from the depths of his being. He understood her now, almost completely. She was going to sacrifice her youth and an unknown number of years to the care of her father. And she thought she was going to do it alone.

She was wrong.

Mortal he might be, but there was a great deal he could do to make life easier, happier, for Jane and her father. She had finally started to trust him, yet as soon as he had begun to reassure her, to broach the subject of their future together, she had cut him off with a single, chilling negative. He hadn't won her yet. There was one more barrier, one last barrier, to overcome, and it was this which made his understanding of Jane incomplete. He had the answer, the missing piece, but he still didn't know where it fitted into the picture.

He thought hard about his meeting with Gerald, and a slow smile broke out on his face. He had a strong feeling that in Gerald Winters he had an ally. An ally was something Adam was very much in need of at the moment. He had every intention of talking to Gerald . . .

CHAPTER EIGHT

IT was raining. It had rained almost constantly since she'd stepped off the plane in the very early hours of Sunday morning. It seemed that during the week Jane had been away the seasons had changed rapidly. October had slipped into November. The autumn had gone and winter had set in. If the temperature was anything to go by, the months ahead would be cold, depressing, hard. It was a close description of the way Jane was feeling.

She shivered as she stepped into the warmth of the foyer. The usual crowd of people were waiting for the lift, the usual good mornings were exchanged and as she walked into the offices of Brinkman, Clayton and Brinkman, the receptionist smiled her usual smile. It was Wednesday. And life was continuing in its normal fashion.

Almost.

For Jane, life could never be quite the same again, now she was in love with Adam Francis. She shook herself mentally, impressing on her mind for the millionth time that she must not think like that, must not think of Adam at all. She was trying to harden herself, to protect herself from her own feelings, but it was a pathetic, futile thing to attempt. After all, she had thought herself protected before, but Adam Francis had ploughed his way through her barriers— and walked straight into her heart. Her blood. Her every waking thought. She had to face it: he would be there for a long time to come.

She should never have gone to San Pablo. She should never have allowed herself the pleasure of being in his arms. She should never have allowed herself to trust him. Wouldn't she ever learn? How could she have allowed this to happen when she knew that nothing in life could really be relied upon?

'Morning, Jane. Rotten day, isn't it?' The temp's voice broke into her thoughts. Mr Brinkman had hired her while Jane was away, and Jane was very relieved she had been willing to stay on for a second week in order to help clear up the backlog of work. She was good. In fact, Jane had every intention of recommending her to Mr Brinkman as a possible replacement.

'Good morning, Sally. Is the boss free?'

Sally's attractive face creased into a frown. She was about ten years older than Jane, auburn-haired, with a vivacious look which matched her personality. 'Mrs Hoffman's with him. You made the appointment yourself, yesterday afternoon.'

'Oh, yes.' Jane felt slightly embarrassed. She kept doing things like this, forgetting things. In the past few days she had done stupid things, too. Like forgetting her watch yesterday morning, like putting the sugar bowl in the fridge last night. Gerald had found it there, and had pulled her leg about it for a good five minutes.

But he'd been surprisingly uninquisitive. He had asked her how she'd liked the Caribbean, and she had told him all about the sights she had seen and the unusual food she had eaten. She had braced herself for questions about Adam, she had even rehearsed what she would tell him, but Gerald hadn't asked what had happened between herself and Adam on a personal level. Much to Jane's relief.

In fact, Gerald was currently almost the last of her worries. He looked better than he had looked for months, and was in good spirits. Jane attributed it to her return; he had overdone things while she had been away, and was obviously very glad to have her home again.

As soon as the boss was free, Jane went in to see him and recommended him to talk to Sally about the possibility of her taking over Jane's job.

'She's good, Mr Brinkman. You've seen her work, and she has a very nice manner on the telephone.' Jane looked at him hopefully. She had given Mr Brinkman only one week's notice when by rights she should have given him two. She felt guilty about it, but she wouldn't budge an inch. She had no intention of being around when Adam Francis came to stay for six months. She had to get out of his orbit—for ever.

'It would solve a lot of problems.' Mr Brinkman sighed. 'But Sally's been temping for over a year. I don't know whether she's interested in taking a permanent job.'

'I haven't asked her,' Jane admitted. 'I thought the question should come from you. But I know she likes it here.'

'Look, you know my feelings about this thing. I don't want to lose you. Won't you reconsider?'

'Absolutely not.'

'Won't you at least tell me your reasons for leaving me?'

Jane smiled at the 'me'. Mr Brinkman was a very sweet man. 'As I told you on Monday, I have——'

'You have personal reasons. Yes, yes, I can see that's all I'm going to get out of you. I'm not daft, Jane. I know Adam's at the bottom of this—blast him! I'm going to tackle him when I see him, you know.'

'Well, he'll be over next week, if that's what you wish to do.' She said it casually, wanting him to think she couldn't care less. 'It's your prerogative, I suppose.'

John Brinkman chuckled inwardly. He'd never seen Jane blushing before. He thought he must be getting old, or something. He'd been very slow on the uptake. He'd only just realised why it had to be Jane who acted as courier to the Caribbean. And he'd only just realised why she was giving only one week's notice. She thought she was taking evasive action. Foolish girl! Furthermore, she seemed to have no idea that Adam Francis had arrived in London over an hour ago . . . Oh, well! At least he felt better now, knowing he was losing his secretary for the nicest possible reason.

'Mr Brinkman? Will you think it over, then, about Sally?'

'Yes. Leave it with me.'

Jane got out of his office as fast as possible. She was

very embarrassed. She wished she could leave Brinkman's today, but that would be really unfair. There were only two more days to go, and she wanted to teach Sally as much as she could in that time.

At four in the afternoon, she and Sally stopped work and had a well earned cup of coffee. The backlog was diminishing gradually. A little before five, Jane switched off her typewriter and went to the ladies' room. She was exhausted, and glad of it. Maybe she'd sleep tonight . . .

As she approached her office, she heard Sally's voice, pitched very high with irritation, indignation. 'I've just told you! Mr Brinkman's gone out to a meeting. If you'd like to make an appointment . . .'

Jane put on a spurt, flung open the office door—and stopped dead in her tracks. His presence seemed to fill the room. In a heavy black overcoat his shoulders looked broader than ever. His hair was wild, his eyes like green ice, cold, penetrating, and his face was a tight mask of anger. 'You! Get your coat on. You're coming with me.'

The fury in his voice, the shock of seeing him, rendered Jane speechless. For a moment she couldn't even move. She was paralysed by her own ambivalence. She wanted to run towards him, to run away from him—and she was too frightened to do either.

Even Sally looked frightened now. She was standing behind her desk, as if it would protect her from the man who had burst in on her. 'Jane . . .?' Her eyes flicked nervously from one person to the other.

'It—it's all right, Sally,' Jane managed. 'This—gentleman—is a client.'

Adam Francis advanced on her threateningly. 'I said get your coat on!'

Jane backed away from him, reaching for her coat, her bag. There would be no arguing with him. She'd never seen him like this before and she was not about to defy him. His fingers closed over her arm like steel bars and he virtually marched her out of the office, leaving the bewildered Sally open-mouthed.

The Rolls was parked on double yellow lines. It was the height of the City rush hour and there was a traffic warden hurrying towards the car. The driving door was open, overhanging the pavement, and the engine was quietly ticking over.

As soon as they got on to the street, Jane tried to bolt. She had no idea why he was so furious with her, and she didn't want to find out. She just panicked. 'Let go of me! Let *go*!' She flung all her weight away from him, but the hand on her arm didn't even move.

'Get in,' he ordered, half lifting her and half throwing her on to the passenger seat.

The traffic warden didn't even approach Adam. Some passers-by were smirking, some giving them a wide berth. Jane felt foolish, humiliated—and incensed. 'What the hell do you think you're doing?' As he slipped in beside her, she tried to open her door. It had locked itself. Before she had a chance to fumble with the handle, she was suddenly thrown back against her seat as the car pulled away at a rapid but effortless speed.

'Where are you taking me?' she demanded.

Adam turned left.

'I've got to get home. Let me out of here this minute! I'm not going anywhere with you. Do you understand?'

Adam turned left again.

'What *is* this all about? Where are you taking me? I warn you, Adam, I'm getting very, very angry!'

'Shut up,' he said, turning right.

Jane gave up and fell silent. They didn't drive for long. They pulled up at a house with a rather splendid-looking front door in a fashionable mews in Mayfair.

She was escorted from the car just as she'd been escorted into it, like a prisoner. Adam let go of her as soon as he closed the front door behind them. This was obviously the house he had rented; Jane had an impression of a very masculine room with brown leather furniture, a faint smell of furniture polish, but that was all. Even that was tinged with a haze of red. She turned on him viciously, but Adam spoke first.

He towered over her, his height, the blackness of his clothes and the ice in his eyes intimidating her so that she actually cowered. Her emotions went full circle, from fear to anger to fear.

'You've handed your notice in. *Why*?'

'I—I—because I want a change, that's all.'

'That's the wrong answer.' The deep voice bellowed at her, making her flinch. 'Now let's have the truth!'

'I—it's it is true,' she stammered. 'I feel the need for a change. N-new stimulus.'

'Stimulus!' He picked up the word as if she couldn't have said anything worse. Then he backed away from her, as if he couldn't trust himself not to slap her, his fists clenching and unclenching.

Jane's shoulders relaxed and dropped with relief because he'd moved away. But she stood, motionless, her hands over her hips as though she had said something wicked.

Adam flung his overcoat over a chair, his hand reaching up to rub the back of his neck. 'Stimulus, eh? Now we're getting a little closer to the truth.' He spun round to face her, pointing an accusing finger. 'All right, then I'll tell you why you're leaving Brinkman's. Things are hotting up a little, aren't they? There are too many people involved now, and you're about to be found out. You want to get out before your secret life's discovered and the gossip starts!'

She just looked at him, dumbfounded. She hadn't the faintest idea what he was talking about.

'I had lunch with Paul Meekins today . . .' He watched her face closely, seeing her loss of colour. 'You might well look like that, Jane. You've never had a date with him in your life!'

'I—I never actually told you I had.'

She might as well have not spoken. Adam's voice cracked like a whip. 'And that's not all I learned. I know all about your other man, Jane. Believe me, it did not make for pleasant listening.'

'No!' She ventured nearer, unable to believe her ears. 'Paul—Paul wouldn't gossip about me. He doesn't know——'

'He would, and he did! Admittedly, only after I'd plied him with a few drinks. Boy, was that money well spent! Paul's got it really bad over you. He's shattered because you've handed in your notice. He was fool enough to think his patient waiting would pay off. He's got it bad over you—despite what you're doing!'

Her mind spun confusedly. David Boyd—Paul—the scene he had witnessed in the wine bar. 'But David—I mean, Paul doesn't know the—he doesn't know——'

'David Boyd—*your lover*? No, he doesn't actually know him. But he knows him by sight. He knows *of* him. Solicitors know other solicitors, Jane, just as doctors know other doctors. That can't be news to you. He knows Boyd is married—with three children!'

'Oh, my goodness!' Jane turned away, appalled by the look in Adam's eyes, appalled to think that all these months Paul had believed she was having an affair with a married man! Never for a moment had it occurred to her that Paul had *identified* her ex-boss! A wave of shame engulfed her and she buried her face in her hands.

'Yes, you might well hide your face.' Adam swore then, stalking around the room as if he wanted to smash everything in sight. Including Jane.

She started trembling as he swore at her again with

words she had never have expected him to use in front
of her. But she couldn't blame him for losing every
ounce of respect. Not after what he'd been told!

'You're certainly the deceptive one,' he hissed. 'Not
at all what you seemed to be, are you?' He laughed
hollowly. 'Of course, I always knew that much. But I
didn't think this lot would be at the bottom of the
mystery. Even your father has no idea about your
secret life, has he? Why should he suspect when he
thinks you're going out with Paul? You've been using
Paul—and maybe a few others for all I know—as
alibis, excuses for your clandestine nights out with a
married man twice your age! But you weren't that
clever, Jane. Your mistake was being seen in public,
having an intimate little chat over a bottle of wine.
What happens next on these evenings of yours? After
Boyd's wined you and dined you? No doubt he takes
you to a motel. Tell me, do you always use the same
one, or do you ring the changes, in case of gossip?'

Jane shrank inwardly as he went on, wishing the
floor would open up and swallow her. But why
shouldn't he believe all this? She'd tied herself up so
neatly with her own ludicrous cover-up job. She
didn't want Adam to believe this of her, she couldn't
bear the shame and disgust in his eyes. Yet she had
been handed the perfect solution. She had never been
able to run from Adam Francis, but this was the
perfect way out! It would make the final, disgusting
turn-off.

'Yes!' she shouted. 'That's right. I told you there
was someone else, but you wouldn't listen. David's my
ex-boss. Our affair started when I worked for him. I
moved to Brinkman's to protect him from office
gossip—and I've been seeing him ever since.'

Adam Francis looked fit to kill. 'You admit it, then.
All of this?'

'Of course I admit it!' she shrieked. 'What ever

are you so mad about, anyway? Are you angry because someone beat you to it? Are you angry because someone else is giving me what you wanted to give me?'

She saw him advancing on her, but she couldn't seem to stop herself. She was afraid, of him, of what she was saying ... but she was more afraid of the extent of her love for him. 'I have my needs like everyone else. David gives me everything I need, and it suits us both! There are no ties in it. It's nice and convenient. He doesn't want a divorce, and I don't want——'

Adam's powerful hands closed on her shoulders and she yelped with pain. 'Very nice!' he spat. 'How very nice! Well, I reckon I'm due for a piece of that. I reckon you owe me something for all that teasing, all that provocation you gave me!' He yanked her towards him so roughly that she lost her balance. Then he was half dragging her towards the settee. Cold fear gripped her as his words penetrated. Her legs buckled, but Adam picked her up and dropped her on to the leather cushions.

'Adam!' Her scream was cut off in mid-air as his mouth claimed hers savagely. She fought with all the power her terror gave to her, but she was naturally no match. She couldn't even budge him. His hands were under her jacket, roaming her body rapidly, crudely.

As her hands beat against his back, Adam's lips moved to her throat. 'Debts, Jane,' he said hoarsely. 'I always pay them and I always collect on them. I'm the fool who fell for your frightened virgin act. I'm the fool who fell in love with you!'

'Stop it!' she screamed. She screamed again, long and loud, as she felt the catch on her bra open and his hands closed roughly over her breasts.

'What's the matter, Jane? This is what you like, isn't it? No ties, no emotion—just sex. Isn't this what

David Boyd gives you? Don't you know the old adage?'

He said something so vulgar that she cried out for shame, gasping for breath. Her adrenalin petered out and left her limp, sobbing, her hands flaying weakly against his chest. 'No, no, no. It isn't true. It isn't true!'

'What, Jane. *What*?'

'I can't!' she sobbed. 'It's not true! I'm not like that . . . ooh!'

Even before her pitiful moan had ended, she was cradled in his arms. She lay against Adam like a rag doll, the tears streaming down her face, sobbing so violently it seemed she would never breathe normally again.

'Hush,' he whispered. 'Hush, darling, hush. It's all over. It's all right.'

She felt the coolness of his fingers, soothing against her flushed face, as he moved her head back gently. 'It's all right, darling. I'll never put you through anything like that again.'

She looked at him like a lost child, and clung to him desperately as a fresh bout of tears filled her eyes.

Adam let her cry it out. This was the final barrier dissolving. His beloved Jane was a very strong-minded girl—a misguided, confused innocent. He'd tried everything in the book in order to reach her, with so little reward. It had been time for a little shock treatment.

'I love you, my darling girl,' he crooned. 'There's nothing to be afraid of now. Nothing. Not ever. Oh, Jane, what tangled webs . . . And all because you were afraid to love and be loved. Don't you know that love is the most precious thing in the world? Ah, my darling, of course you do—so much of this was for your father's sake, wasn't it? You crazy, crazy darling!'

He went on, reassuring her, holding her, rocking

her gently back and forth until she was all cried out. She started hiccupping, looking up at him as if it alarmed her. Adam smiled, though his heart twisted inside him. There it was, in her eyes—the love he had waited so long to see there. She would never be able to hide it from him again.

'All right now.' He eased her back against the settee. 'Time for a cup of coffee, I think.' He left the room, smiling as Jane blew her nose loudly.

It was about all she had the energy to do. There was no fight left in her, not in any sense. She would, she knew, be putty in his hands now. And she didn't mind at all. Hadn't he warned her often enough that she'd never be able to run away from him? He must have known all along that she didn't really want to. Although she'd only just realised that herself.

Adam came back with two steaming mugs of coffee. 'Here, drink this and you'll feel better.'

'Adam, I—I'm so ashamed.' She couldn't look at him as he sat down beside her.

'There's no need to be. I didn't tell Paul anything. He did all the talking, I just listened. He's still crazy about you, despite what he believes.'

'Oh, I didn't mean that! I don't care about that. I—I'm ashamed because—because of you.'

'I'm glad to hear it,' he said. But his eyes were smiling, telling her she must never be ashamed with him, that there was nothing he wouldn't understand. 'It means you care.'

'I ... Oh, Adam, you know how much I care. You've known all along.'

'Yes,' he said softly, 'long before you did.' He tilted her face up to his, forcing her to meet his eyes. He kissed her very lightly on the lips, her nose, her tear-streaked face. 'Can you tell me now? Can you say those all-important words?'

Those all-important words. It had been such a long,

long time since she'd said them to someone. 'I love you,' she whispered.

'I'm sorry, I didn't quite hear you.' He put his arms around her, holding her so close she could feel the beat of his heart. She clung to him, revelling in his strength, his support, his constancy . . . his love for her. She told him again how she loved him, though she was inwardly still a little afraid. Not of Adam, but of the power of her own emotions, the fear that it might not last.

'Jane, let me bring you up to date on what's happened.' Adam moved away from her slightly. Holding her close was too much of a distraction, and they had to talk now. 'I've been disengaging myself from my American work, as you know. I tied things up as quickly as possible because I wanted to get back to London, to be with you.

'I met young Meekins here at two this afternoon. He handed over the keys, asked if I approved of the place. I took him out to a late lunch by way of thanking him for his work on the Birmingham project, and you know the rest. I think you'll understand how I felt when his tongue loosened and I got the story of David Boyd from him.'

He took hold of Jane's hands. She was still trembling. 'I wasn't angry, not for a minute. Because I knew better. Meekins had swallowed the story of another man, but I never did. As for the idea of Boyd being your lover . . .' He laughed, genuinely, as if it were a crazy notion. 'You've never had a lover, Jane. I know that as well as you do. In fact, you've never before been loved, not in the way you deserve to be loved . . .'

Jane closed her eyes. A fresh bout of tears was threatening. He was right, of course.

'. . . Which brings us to Billy.'

Her eyes flew open. Her breath caught in her throat.

She snatched her hands from Adam's grasp, filled with panic. There was only one person from whom Adam could have got Billy's name. Dear heaven, what had Adam done...? 'You've seen my father!'

Adam's eyes narrowed speculatively. Her response was alarming. 'Ssh, darling. It's all right—it's all right. I've told you you have nothing to worry about, haven't I? Not now. I've told you there's nothing we can't handle?'

She nodded numbly, trying to trust him completely, *completely*. But her heart was beating frantically. Was it here, now, that everything would go wrong?

'As soon as I got through Heathrow I went to see Gerald. I spent the entire morning with him. For heaven's sake, don't look so alarmed! I didn't tell him anything that might upset him, nothing at all. On the contrary. It was he who mentioned Billy, though I was about to. I had every intention of finding out from Gerald who it was who'd hurt you in the past, since I couldn't find out from you.'

Jane went limp with relief. Gerald would, of course, have volunteered the information. He approved very much of Adam. 'What did he tell you?'

'As much as he knows. That you'd known Billy for a long time. That you were engaged to him. That the engagement was broken not long after it became official.' He took hold of her hands again, noticing they'd grown cold. 'The story's incomplete, Jane. I want your version of it now.'

Jane sighed from the depths of her being, a great, shuddering sigh of relief. Her words came out quietly but hurriedly. 'I had known Billy nearly all my life, though it wasn't until we were teenagers that we—that we became friends, if you like. His family had lived in our avenue almost as long as my parents. We all knew each other and got on well.

'When I was in secretarial college, my mother died.

I was eighteen. Billy was away at university and we'd been seeing each other during the holidays, just as friends, really. When ... when my mother died, he was very supportive. He wrote to me every day, he took me out during the holidays. He finished university at the same time I finished college. He was three years older than I, and very bright. We both got good jobs, and during the following year we grew to love each other. He—he proposed. I was just turned twenty when we got engaged. We ... we set the wedding date for the week of my twenty-first birthday.'

She broke off, sighing again. But there was no pain. She knew only relief that she was able, at last, to tell Adam. She got to her feet, restless, her hands fluttering nervously to her throat as Adam waited, patiently. 'We'd been engaged two months when ... when Daddy's illness was diagnosed. His illness overtook him swiftly. This, just two years after Mummy died ...'

She turned away, holding on to the mantelpiece for support. 'Daddy was so ... he seemed to lose all his interest in life. He was still grieving, ill. I was so ... I felt ... But there was the comfort of Billy. And he was so good to Daddy. He really liked him, I thought. I thought also that I had his love—his support.'

She turned to face Adam then, with a long, searching look that spoke volumes. 'In our relationship, we seemed to have no problems. He seemed to be so fond of my father, we both had good jobs, earning good money. Then ... then three weeks after we learned Daddy's prognosis, Billy broke off our engagement. At first, he gave me an excuse, he said marriage was not for him, after all, that it would stand in the way of his career. Finally he told me the truth: that he didn't want ... didn't want the burden of a father-in-law who was going ... who was getting ...'

Adam was on his feet, reaching for her. But Jane held up a hand, shook her head. 'It's all right—I'm okay. It doesn't hurt any more, though at the time, I was——'

'He didn't love you enough,' Adam said quietly.

'At the time, I was sick with disgust. I couldn't understand him. Obviously, my father knows nothing of this. He never knew the truth. Can you imagine how it would make him feel? As things are, he hates the idea of becoming a burden. I told him Billy had fallen in love with someone else. I couldn't say I'd broken it off, because he'd have thought I'd done it for his sake. So I couldn't tell him that, any more than I could tell him the truth. The—the trouble is that for a long time afterwards, Daddy thought I was still hurting over Billy. He still does, I think, though I've tried ... Of course, I *was* hurting at first. My word, when I think of Billy now, I *hate* him!'

'Don't hate, Jane. You lost nothing by losing Billy. He didn't love you *enough*. Come on, sit down.' Adam took hold of her, led her back to the settee. 'Darling, there are a few things you still don't seem to understand—about Gerald, about yourself. You know, I have a lot of respect for your father. He's a wise man. He and I had a long talk, and while he doesn't *know* what happened between you and Billy, he suspects that——'

'No! Oh, Adam, no! Don't say that! Don't tell me he——'

'Jane, please. Will you just relax and hear me out? No, he hasn't guessed the truth, I'm not telling you that. But he does suspect that you've made up your mind never to get involved again. After all, as far as he's concerned, there's only been an occasional date with Paul. For the two years prior to that, you saw no one, you never went out. But Paul—your attempt at putting your father off the scent—wasn't good enough. Gerald knows you're devoted to him, that you want to give him all your time, your youth. Jane, he doesn't want this. He told me himself today.'

'But he needs me! And later on he'll need——'

'Yes, darling.' Adam smiled, understanding her far better than she understood herself. She had a lot of growing to do, and growing was never easy. 'Obviously he'll need looking after. But you don't have to give up on life and live like a nun in order to do it. Those were Gerald's words, not mine. Naturally, I'm in full agreement with him. And when I told him I intend to marry you, he was absolutely delighted!'

Jane should, of course, have seen it coming. In a way, she had. But actually hearing the words, hearing the mention of marriage, made her heart leap with panic as well as pleasure. 'Marriage? Marriage ... Adam, I—I don't know what to say!'

'Say yes,' he grinned. 'Say you love me, that you want to spend the rest of your life with me.'

Jane's fingers went up to her temples. It was all happening so quickly. This whirlwind romance, this proposal, it was all too wonderful to believe. But it was happening. 'I—don't know whether I'm ready ...' Her voice trailed off. She loved Adam so much, but for such a long time she had trained herself never to hope, never to think that ... 'I'm ... Darling, this is all happening so quickly, my mind's in a spin. I love you, you know that. I—I don't even know why I'm hesitating.'

'I do.' He drew her close. 'And this is where you don't understand yourself. You've been locked up behind your barriers for so long that you've lost touch with yourself. Jane, the night I met you, I told you you tried to hide your femininity. It goes deeper than that. You try to hide your personality, your real personality. Think back to that first day on San Pablo, when we went touring. You were yourself then, the self you've forgotten. You were young, happy, relaxed. And very beautiful. You were the person I saw in you when I first looked into your eyes. That's the person you'll be again, when you're my wife. When you've finally accepted that there's nothing to be afraid of. When you finally trust me completely.'

Tawny, almond-shaped eyes were looking at him. Her dark lashes were still damp from her tears. She knew she was hearing the truth. She understood, yet she didn't understand. Not fully. Not yet. Adam took hold of her tenderly, knowing there was sufficient trust for him to explain further. 'Jane, think carefully about what I say. In a way, you see, you've been using your father as an excuse. Granted, he needs you. But I am not Billy. I'm genuinely fond of your father. Further, I'm a very wealthy man, and you must realise that I can make life much easier for him. I shall see that he gets the best treatment. And he can make it to San Pablo, with help—we discussed that today. He can relax there and spend time in the sun, have the best of everything. There'll be people to look after him, besides you and me. You and me, Jane. Gerald will have both of us.'

'Oh, Adam ...' She was choked, loving him, wanting him. 'I'm not comparing you with Billy—don't ever think that. There's no comparison in any way at all. It's just that I have to talk to Daddy first, alone. I have to be sure he's happy about this. Do you understand? He's so unselfish, you see. I must be absolutely *sure* this is what he wants.'

'It is, Jane.' Adam's voice was firm but gentle. 'But I won't ask you for your answer now. If you trusted me completely, you'd take my word for it that he's happy and tell me we'll marry before the week is out. And that, my darling, is really why you hesitate. You don't trust me fully. This is the damage that Billy did to you, the scars he left on you. This is where, in part, you've been using your father as an excuse never to get involved with a man. But the crux of the matter is that you feared you wouldn't be loved enough. *Enough*, Jane. You still fear it. Billy's jilting you knocked your confidence in yourself *as a woman*. I love you enough to take on the whole world in order to make you mine. But you don't see that yet. I can only show you with time. With patience, understanding and demonstration, I'll prove to you that I love you completely.

'So talk to your father. Satisfy yourself that he's delighted about our marriage. Heaven knows I'm in a hurry to make you my wife, but I can wait another day or so.' He smiled at the look on her face. She was trying so hard to understand all he'd said. But the growing process had only just been set in motion. He remembered a time, many years ago, when someone older had tried to explain a few things to him about life, about his own motivations. The seeds had been planted, just as he was planting them now in Jane's mind, but it had been quite a while before those seeds had blossomed, before he had fully understood.

He offered Jane a drink then. She had had quite enough to cope with for one night. 'I'm not sure what Meekins bought in for me, but I'll——'

'No, don't bother. I must get home now.' Jane looked at her watch. 'Good grief, it's almost half past seven! Adam, I must go—now! Daddy will be wondering what's happened to me.'

'Relax!' Adam laughed. 'He knows you're with me. I told him I was taking you out to dinner tonight. He thinks I'm proposing to you right now over a bottle of something special. Are you hungry, darling? Shall we go out and eat?'

'Ugh, I couldn't!' She sat down again. She was far too excited to eat. Excited and anxious; her stomach felt as if it had been tied in knots. 'But I'll take you up on that drink. If you've got brandy, I'll have some—a big one!'

'I'll join you.' He poured himself a stiff Scotch, lit a cigarette and relaxed fully for the first time that day. With his glass raised, he toasted Gerald. 'You know, he wasn't at all surprised to see me today, Jane.'

'Really?'

'Not a bit. He said he'd been wondering when I'd turn up on his doorstep.'

'I don't understand.' Though she was quite bemused, Jane laughed with him.

'You underestimate his powers of observation, darling.'

'I think I underestimated both of you,' Jane smiled wryly. 'Did he explain himself?'

Laughing green eyes did their best to look mysterious. 'Oh, he just mentioned your peculiar behaviour these last few days, said he reckoned that when a girl starts putting sugar in the fridge, she's in love.'

'How embarrassing!' she giggled. 'He must have had you weighed up pretty well, too.'

'Pretty well. Indeed.'

They pulled up outside Jane's home about an hour later. Adam took her in his arms, kissing her tenderly, lastingly. 'I'm loath to let you out of my sight. It's just as well you told old John you were leaving your job. With a bit of luck, we can get married on Saturday. Would you mind getting married in a register——'

'Adam!'

'Oh, go on then—shoo! I'll give you an hour or so, then I'll come back and we can celebrate properly.'

'You'll do no such thing,' Jane admonished. 'You'd be here till three in the morning, if I allowed that. And I do have two more days to work through. Phone me at work in the morning.'

Adam put his hand on his heart. 'Jane! How can you

do this to me? Let's compromise, I'll phone you in a couple of hours.'

'All right.'

He put his hands on either side of her face, happy with what he saw in her eyes; more than happy, he was ecstatic. 'Go now.' His voice was thick with emotion. 'Or I'll keep you locked up in here with me for ever. Do you fancy making love in the back of a Rolls?'

'*Goodnight*, Adam.' Jane got out of the car, laughing gaily. She was laughing at herself, remembering how she had said a very firm goodnight to him here once before, not so very long ago. How much had happened since then! How quickly lives could change in the space of a few weeks.

She didn't bother taking the lift. She ran up the stairs to her first floor flat as if there were wings on her heels.

'Daddy? I'm home!' The hope, the happiness in her voice was something she couldn't manage to conceal. 'I'll put the kettle on.' She popped her head round the living room door. Gerald was sound asleep.

The room was in semi-darkness and he was lying with his feet up on the sofa. He was smiling in his sleep, and Jane laughed softly, ducking back into the kitchen. She made tea, humming to herself, and stacked a plate with biscuits, wondering whether her father had eaten.

'Wake up, Pop! Tea's made.' Jane put down the tea tray and gave her father a gentle nudge. It was only then that she looked at him properly. His face was a strange colour; what she'd thought was a smile on his face was in fact a grimace of pain. And Gerald Winters was not asleep.

CHAPTER NINE

'JANE? Jane love, we'll have to go back to your flat now.' Mrs Graham's voice was trembling. 'I'll stay with you, dear. But we'll have to go next door. I—I haven't got a spare bed in here.'

'I can't go in there.' It was all Jane could manage to say. Everything seemed to be hazy, and her voice sounded strange to her own ears.

It was almost midnight, and they'd taken Jane into her neighbour's flat so she couldn't witness what was happening. Gerald had been taken to hospital. His G.P., Dr Leonard, had gone with him in the ambulance. But nobody could help Gerald now. He had died of a heart attack, and all that remained to be done were the medical formalities.

'Jane . . .?'

'I can't go in there, Mrs Graham. I can't walk into that empty flat.'

Mrs Graham nodded. Her chubby, elderly face was pink from crying. She understood Jane's feelings only too well. 'Then I'll go and get your things. You can sleep on my sofa.' She patted Jane's hand reassuringly. 'I'll be right back.'

Jane heard the front door open. She heard voices in the corridor, but she couldn't make out what was being said. She was staring into space, understanding where she was, what was being said to her—but she couldn't seem to respond properly. Everything seemed to be far away, distorted.

The voices came closer. She heard Mrs Graham's protest for the umpteenth time, 'But he was all right a few hours ago. He seemed fine. He was having a cup of tea in my kitchen only a few hours ago. I can't believe what's happened. I just can't believe it!'

Then there was a hand on her shoulder and a voice with a soft, West Country accent speaking to her. 'Jane? I want you to stay with Mrs Graham tonight. Mrs Graham, I'd appreciate a cup of tea, if you'd be so kind . . .'

'Dr Leonard . . .'

'It's all right, dear. Take it easy. Let me look at you.'

Warm fingers encircled Jane's wrist. She was looking into the kindly eyes of the man who had brought her into the world, the man who had been both doctor and friend to Gerald for many years. Somewhere in her head, or perhaps it was a long way in the distance—she couldn't tell—a bell was ringing. The scrutiny of Dr Leonard's eyes continued. She felt his fingers on her cheeks, pulling gently beneath her lashes. The bell stopped. His face moved out of focus and in again.

A small bottle of tablets was pressed into her hand. 'Here, I want you to take two of these tonight. They'll help you sleep. I'm giving you enough for three nights, Jane.'

Jane nodded. Her mind was functioning well enough. She had no intention of taking the tablets, but she wouldn't tell him that. She couldn't tell him that. She was having difficulty in saying anything at all.

'I've telephoned your Aunt Margaret. She's coming down from Scotland on the early train tomorrow. All right, Jane? Jane?'

'Yes. That'll be fine.' It seemed to be a satisfactory response; the doctor moved away from her.

Then there was Mrs Graham's voice: 'Jane, there's a gentle——'

'Jane!' Adam Francis was standing behind Mrs

Graham, towering over her as she hovered in the doorway. 'Darling, I—Mrs Graham's just told me. Darling, I'm so sorry, so very, very sorry——' He eased Mrs Graham out of his way, came hurrying towards Jane. 'When I phoned you and there was no reply, I came straight over. I—Oh, darling . . .'

'Don't touch me.'

The hands which were about to take hold of her froze. Then they reached for her again.

'I said *don't touch me*. Get out! Get out of my sight, Adam!'

Everything snapped into place. Everything hit her at once. There was no more distortion, only clarity, clarity, clarity. 'This is your fault!' she screamed. 'Where was I when my father needed me? With *you*! Where was I a few hours ago, when my presence here would have saved his life? Being kidnapped, attacked, by *you*! Where was I all last week—the last week of Daddy's life? On the other side of the world. Because *you* tricked me into going there!'

She was shouting at the top of her voice, her hands beating against Adam's chest. He did nothing to stop her. He just stared at her, unable to believe what he'd heard.

'Jane, Jane!' It was Dr Leonard who got hold of her. Mrs Graham just stared, horrified, her hands on either side of her face. And all Adam said was, 'You don't know what you're saying. You don't know what you're saying . . .'

He was ashen, motionless, and for Jane there was a perverse pleasure in seeing him look like that. She wanted him to suffer. She pushed Dr Leonard away so there was nobody between herself and Adam. 'Daddy's dead, and do you know why? Because he gave up on life, that's why! He gave up on life because——'

'Jane, stop this! Can't you see——'

'Keep out of this, Doctor!' She turned viciously on Dr Leonard before turning to Adam again. He was shaking his head in disbelief, repeating the same words he'd said a moment ago.

'I know what I'm saying. You presumed too much, Adam. You had *no right* to speak to Daddy about marriage before I'd given you my answer, before you'd spoken to me——'

'You'd better go, Mr—— You'd better go. This has been a terrible shock, traumatic . . .' The middle-aged doctor tried unsuccessfully to intervene.

Mrs Graham started crying.

'You want my answer?' Jane screamed hysterically. 'Well, here it is—I hate you! I hate you as I've never hated in my life. I——'

Adam caught hold of her flaying arms. 'Jane, your father was happy—happy, I told you——'

'I wouldn't take your word for anything. Get out of my sight!'

'Please, young man. Please go. Leave her with me.'

'It—it's Mr Francis.' Mrs Graham found her voice at last. 'Please go, Mr Francis. She'll be all right with me and the doctor.'

'A heart attack!' Jane screamed. 'Daddy died of a heart attack because of the shock you gave him. Because he thought he was losing me!'

'*Please*, Mr Francis . . .'

Jane continued her abuse as Adam moved reluctantly toward the door. He had no choice but to leave. Dear heaven, he didn't want to leave her now, not now...

'He gave up on life because he thought he was losing me. I was all he had to live for, do you hear me? And where was I when he was dying? Where was I?'

'*Please*, Mr Francis . . .

As Adam was ushered out of Jane's sight by a frantic Mrs Graham, the room shifted sickeningly. A moment later all Jane knew was blackness, total blackness.

On the day of the funeral, Adam was there. He had parked by the cemetery railings, a short distance behind the cars which were lined up waiting to take the mourners home. He was watching, waiting. Nobody had asked him to come, but he couldn't keep away.

A freezing wind was howling, as if in protest at the scene taking place. Despite the protection of the car, Adam had never felt so cold. It was a coldness which came from inside. He had to try—just once more he had to try to reach Jane.

He had called at Mrs Graham's flat on the morning after Gerald's death, only to be turned away by a firm but sympathetic Dr Leonard, who had been keeping a close eye on Jane. Over the next couple of days he had called at Jane's flat, too, where she was now being looked after by her aunt, her mother's sister. On his third visit, the aunt had finally let him see Jane, had let him into her room, and he had talked to her. He had talked and talked. But he had no way of knowing whether she had even heard him. She was in shock. She was responding to nothing and no one.

He drew deeply on a cigarette, watching as Jane and her small entourage approached the waiting cars. Then he went to her. Friends and relatives moved on in order to give them a moment's privacy. All but Dr Leonard, who stood just a few yards to one side.

'Jane?'

She responded—but she did so by turning her back on him. Adam moved in front of her. 'Jane, after today I won't bother you again, but I want you to know . . . I want you to know, I'll be waiting. I had to come here. Darling, I had to come, to pay my respects and to tell you I'll be waiting for you. When you're over this, and you will get over it, I'll be waiting. You must come to me, Jane. Come to me. Jane, Jane my darling, I'll be waiting——'

'You can wait till hell freezes over. Get away from me.' Her words were spoken without a trace of feeling, and as Adam looked into her eyes, he saw—nothing. There was no emotion registered there. Nothing at all. And it was infinitely more terrifying than if he had seen hatred. That, at least, would have been some sort of emotion.

She walked away from him.

Dr Leonard shook his head, motioning Adam to stay where he was. He took hold of Jane's arm and led her to the car, telling the driver to move on.

Adam watched as the cars pulled away. He felt the sympathetic looks from Jane's relatives, but Jane kept her eyes straight ahead of her. She wouldn't even look at him.

'What happens now, Doctor?'

'You wait. I'm afraid that's all you can do.' The older man's scrutiny was keen, understanding. 'It's not much consolation to you, Mr Francis, but what just happened was a positive step. Jane responded, at least. Those were the first words she's spoken since she passed out just after you left last Wednesday. The shock of this has been tremendous, traumatic. Only when she breaks down and cries her heart out will the healing time start. In the meantime she can't properly assimilate what's happened. Do you understand?'

'Of course I understand, but to some extent she is aware. She's blaming me for Gerald's death.'

'That's how it looks. She has to place the blame somewhere. She has an enormous feeling of guilt. You heard what she said when she was hysterical: "Where was I when my father was dying...?" She can't handle that guilt—so she's placing it elsewhere. We know nobody's guilty, nobody is to blame, but Jane doesn't know it yet. Someone has to take the responsibility for what's happened.'

Adam nodded and Dr Leonard patted his shoulder reassuringly. 'Her mother's younger sister is taking her back to Scotland. She'll be all right there. Miss MacKenzie is a nursing Sister. I've spoken with her. She'll know how to cope with this, don't worry. I want Jane out of that flat for a while, and she needs to have someone with her.'

'It should be *me*,' Adam said thickly. '*I* should be with her now!'

'It *can't* be you.'

'I know that, Doctor! I know!' He looked away, cursing audibly. 'I'm sorry, Doctor. I—it's just—— Have you talked to her?'

'At length. Just as you have. But it's useless at the moment. She hears, but she doesn't listen. I'll talk to her again when she comes back from Scotland.'

'You will? Will you? Will you try to explain——'

'Of course,' Dr Leonard said hastily. 'Of course I will.'

'I gave her a bad time, you know, the night of Gerald's death.'

'I gathered that,' the doctor smiled. 'But it isn't relevant.'

'It is relevant,' Adam insisted. 'I was trying to make her understand a few things about herself, her attitude.'

'That can't be a bad thing.' Dr Leonard was equally firm. He knew all about the change that had taken place in Jane after she had been jilted. 'I've told you, it isn't relevant to Jane's present mental state. At the moment, she probably can't remember anything that happened last Wednesday, prior to her finding her father.'

There was really nothing else to be said. The two men shook hands and Dr Leonard climbed into his car.

Adam bent his shoulders against the wind, his hair flying wildly as he walked into the cemetery. What the doctor said made sense, but he couldn't possibly understand Adam's fears. He wasn't in command of all the facts. When nature's protective anaesthesia lifted and Jane could think again, she would revert to the stage she was at when Adam last talked to her. She had not trusted Adam fully. She had been undecided, about to seek her father's approval before she committed herself to Adam. She had needed to know he was happy.

And Gerald Winters was no longer around to tell her anything.

Adam stood by Gerald's grave, hunched against the freezing wind, cursing himself for his own blunders. Time. Timing. He'd got the timing wrong. There was nothing he could do now. Jane had to come to him. It *had* to be that way now.

But Jane was teetering on an emotional tightrope. The growing process had been arrested. Soon she would fall, and Adam had no idea what would happen then. He knew only that if she took a step in the wrong direction she would never, ever, come to him.

'I'm sorry, Gerald,' he said softly. 'I got the timing wrong. I did what I'd warned myself not to do—I rushed her. Now all we can do is wait. And hope.'

Jane and her Aunt Margaret had the compartment to themselves. From the windows of the train, all Jane could see was snow. White mountains. White sky. As a child, she had seen Scotland in all seasons. She and her parents had taken many holidays there. They had had holidays abroad, too, but they had always gone to Scotland at least once a year, to stay with Aunt Margaret. Gerald had loved the fishing, and Moira had never tired of visiting her homeland.

Travelling through the Highlands again was like

stepping back into the past. Just looking at the mountains brought memories flooding back to her. The only trouble was that flashes of the present kept intervening . . .

They had talked to her, separately, Adam Francis and Dr Leonard. Aunt Margaret should never have let them in. Not when Jane had been helpless, unable to answer back, unable to throw them out. They had lied to her, both of them. She had heard what they'd said, and she had tried hard to blot out their words, but she hadn't succeeded.

Adam had insisted over and over that Gerald had been happy, delighted with the news of the marriage. Obviously he would say that. It suited his own ends. He was guilty, as guilty as Jane, if not more.

Dr Leonard had lied, too. He had told Jane that Gerald had a weak heart, that the condition had been picked up on an E.C.G. test eighteen months ago. It was the first Jane had heard of such a thing. Gerald had never had an E.C.G. He'd have told her if he had.

She didn't feel angry at their lies, though. She didn't *feel* anything. It was curious, being like that. Jane was glad of it. Nothing could touch her now. She was safe. Nothing could hurt her, affect her in any way.

Even when she thought of the funeral, she was unmoved. There had been some of Gerald's friends there, people he used to work with, who had kept in touch after his enforced retirement. Her mother's older sister, Aunt Alice, had been there with her husband. They had driven down from Edinburgh and left immediately afterwards, Aunt Alice in floods of tears.

Aunt Margaret had kept her composure, though. She had done everything; she had even packed Jane's suitcase for her when she announced that she was taking her back to Inverness for a while.

Jane looked over at her aunt. Margaret was her

mother's younger sister, a woman in her mid-forties who had never married. She was so like Moira physically that if Jane narrowed her eyes slightly she could imagine she was looking not at her aunt but at her own mother.

She narrowed her eyes.

Margaret looked up from her book, smiling. 'You're looking at me very strangely, Jane. What are you thinking?'

'That you look so much like Mummy, especially round the eyes. They're so dark, just like Mummy's were. I'm also thinking that the only time I've seen you over the past few years has been at weddings and funerals.'

Margaret skipped over the last comment. 'Keep squinting! Your mother was very beautiful, and you flatter me. Look at all this grey in my hair! If there's a likeness, it begins and ends round the eyes.'

She put down her book, but Jane turned her attention back to the whiteness of the mountains. It was still an effort to talk. Thinking of the past was more comfortable. She went back in her mind to the holidays she had spent touring Scotland. Happy times.

'Jane, I'm going to the buffet car.' Her aunt's voice was an imposition. 'Would you like coffee, a sandwich?'

'No, thank you.'

'We've another two hours to go, and you barely touched your lunch.'

'No. Nothing for me.'

Margaret MacKenzie didn't push it, any more than she would try to draw Jane into conversation. The girl was not ill, she would eat when she was hungry and talk when she was ready. Margaret was only too pleased to see some signs of life in her niece, some responses after her days of total silence. It was too soon to try coaxing her into anything.

They arrived at Inverness a little after eight. It was dark outside and there was six inches of snow on the ground. 'I hope the car starts,' Margaret said as they walked through the brightly lit station.

Jane said nothing. If the car didn't start, Aunt Margaret would think of something. Besides, she didn't really care what happened at the moment. Nothing seemed to matter, nothing at all.

Aunt Margaret lived on the outskirts of Inverness, to the west of the town. They turned off the trunk road and into the winding, dimly lit lane at the end of which stood what used to be the MacKenzie family home, the house where Jane's mother had been brought up with her two sisters. Now Aunt Margaret lived there alone. There were only five houses in the lane, quite a distance from one another. Beyond the houses were miles of open fields and, in the distance, the mountains. It occurred to Jane that life must get very lonely for her aunt.

'I have new neighbours,' Margaret said brightly, almost as if she had read Jane's thoughts. She pointed to the house nearest her own as they drove past. 'No doubt you'll meet them while you're here. Mother, father and five children! The youngest is a terror, but adorable. He calls in to see me often. He's six, young Jimmy, with hair the colour of a carrot!'

'That's nice.'

'And his mother's very kind, neighbourly. I phoned her last night and told her we'd be arriving about now. I asked her to put a match to the fire so we won't have to walk into a cold room. I left a spare key with her— and my dog!'

'Betsy,' Jane murmured. Betsy was her aunt's Border collie. 'I'd forgotten about her.'

'She won't have forgotten you,' Margaret smiled. 'Don't expect too much, though. She's very old now, and quite deaf.'

Jane expected nothing. Nothing in life stayed the same. Nothing could be relied upon. Nothing was constant.

She revised that thought, later, when she was lying in the same bed she had slept in as a youngster, in the same room she had occupied during holidays. This house was the same, big and old and creaky at night. The carpets and furniture were the same, too, straightforward, solid, reliable. Rather like Aunt Margaret. She didn't change. In her long career as a nursing Sister she had probably seen so much that nothing shocked her any more. She had what could only be described as inner strength.

Jane felt herself relax slightly, and it was only when she did so that she realised how tense she'd been. It would be a good thing to stay here for a while. Perhaps some of her aunt's strength would rub off on her.

As if to mock the idea, she felt her body stiffen again. She wouldn't be able to stay here for ever. One day she would have to go back to London. To face that empty flat. To face the present, even the future.

Two hours later, still unable to sleep, she fished in her handbag and finally resorted to taking two of the sleeping pills Dr Leonard had given her.

CHAPTER TEN

'You don't talk like us. And you're not like Margaret.' It was almost an accusation.

Jane looked disdainfully at the red-haired six-year-old. This was his third visit in five days, and his presence was very much an imposition. She wanted to be alone.

Aunt Margaret was at the hospital. She left very
early in the mornings and got home around two. But
Jane hardly noticed whether Margaret was at work or
not, she was so wrapped up in her thoughts. And
during the evening Margaret would sit quietly,
watching television or listening to the radio, or
reading. She didn't pry, she didn't make useless small-
talk, and she didn't put on a false front of
cheerfulness. She just was—quiet, pleasant, strong.

'I know I'm not like Margaret.' Jane spoke sharply
to the skinny little boy. 'And I've told you not to come
here when you know she's at work. Why aren't you in
school, anyway?'

'I've told you,' Jimmy said impatiently, 'I've had
measles and the doctor won't let me go back yet.
Besides, it's Sunday. You don't go to school on
Sunday! I don't know why Margaret goes to the
hospital. My dad doesn't go to work on Sundays.'

'Then go and pester your dad!' Jane snapped. 'If it's
Sunday, you can play with your brothers and sisters.'

It was as if she hadn't spoken. Jimmy just cocked
his head to one side and looked at her curiously.
'Margaret lets me walk with her when she takes Betsy
out. Why don't you? I've seen you taking her for
walks.'

Jane said nothing. She realised that the only way to
get rid of the boy was to keep silent. If he got no
feedback, he'd get bored.

He got bored. He left about five minutes later. Jane
put on her coat and went for a long, long walk.
Without the dog. So she could think without danger of
being disturbed.

It had been illogical, of course, to think Dr Leonard
had lied to her. Unlike Adam, the doctor had no
motive for lying. She sighed deeply, looking round at
the vast open space, noticing for the first time how
very beautiful her surroundings were. She plodded on

through the glistening snow. Perhaps there'd been some sort of mistake . . . That had to be the answer. If Gerald had had a weak heart, he would have told her. He would. If only she'd been there! If only Adam Francis hadn't detained her . . .

She was asleep when her aunt came home, curled up on the chair by the fire. Margaret stood in the doorway, looking at her worriedly. It hadn't hit her yet. Jane had been there almost a week and she hadn't shed a tear, hadn't even mentioned her father's name. Not once.

At least she was eating properly now. Eating, walking and sleeping—without tablets. That was a blessing. If anything, she was sleeping too much. She was tiring herself out, walking for miles, then sleeping as a form of escape.

Margaret left the room quietly. She put the groceries away, peeled the potatoes and went upstairs to make the beds.

Jimmy, undaunted, came back two days later. Jane was in her room. She heard him knocking and made no move to answer the door. Until Betsy started barking loudly and the noise was more than she could bear.

She flung open the front door and immediately blocked the little boy's path. 'What now?'

'Can't I come in?' He looked positively hurt.

'No. Margaret's at work. You know when she'll be home.'

'But I came to see you!'

'Why?' she snapped.

''Cos Mum said I should leave you alone.'

Jane stared at him. 'Then why don't you!'

'I want to know what's wrong with you. Are you ill?'

'Yes,' she sighed. 'Sort of.'

'Is that why you're staying with a nurse?'

'No. Margaret's my aunt—she told you.'

'You look pretty. You don't look ill.'

Jane swore under her breath. He was just standing there, balaclava, wellingtons and all, impervious to the falling snow, watching her as if she were a weird and fascinating specimen. 'Neither do you.'

'I'm better. I can go back to school on Monday. It's not worth it, though, 'cos we'll be stopping for Christmas holidays in two weeks.'

'Go home, Jimmy!' Jane shouted, using every ounce of restraint not to slam the front door shut.

That cured him, finally. He kept away from then on. He didn't even come round on Margaret's day off. Not that Jane actually noticed his absence. By the time Friday came around she had a headache that no amount of walking would help. In the afternoon she accepted a couple of aspirins from her aunt and went to bed.

Margaret called her down for dinner, and it was some time later that Jane actually asked what she'd been trying to ask for days. 'Aunt Margaret, these E.C.G. tests they give in hospitals—are they ever wrong?'

Margaret closed her book and set it aside. 'Wrong?'

'I mean, could the doctors have made a mistake . . . is the reading . . . Dr Leonard told me . . .'

Margaret watched her niece's agitation. She was biting hard on her lip, unable to finish her sentences. But it was time, now, to give her a little push. 'Dr Leonard told you about your father's complication. Yes, he told me about it. It's true, Gerald did have a weak heart. There's no mistake.'

Jane's face paled. She got to her feet, shouting at the top of her voice. 'Why didn't he tell me? Why didn't he *tell* me?'

Margaret had already thought about that. 'I can only assume he was trying to protect you——'

'Protect me? I'm not a child!'

'True. And in my opinion, he should have told you.'

'If I'd known, I'd never have left him alone. Never!'

'Then that's obviously the reason he didn't tell you.' Margaret paused, waiting for the words to register before she said more. 'You had enough to contend with, Jane, knowing about his condition. No doubt he was trying to spare you added worry. Right or wrong, you can't blame your father for wanting to do that.'

Jane shifted about restlessly, her arms in the air. 'I don't blame Daddy for anything! I blame myself! *Myself!*'

Margaret McKenzie sagged with relief. It was out, at last. 'For what?' she asked quietly.

Jane stared at her incredulously. 'For not being there! For not guessing. I saw him looking tired so often. Sometimes he'd look grey. I should have guessed what was wrong!'

'And how were you supposed to differentiate?' Her aunt looked at her levelly. 'Why should you have suspected it was something other than the illness you knew about?'

'Never mind that!' Jane shouted illogically. 'I could have saved his life if I'd been with him. I could have got help for him!'

'No, Jane. Your father was very, very weak. He couldn't have survived even the mildest attack. I know what I'm talking about, love.'

It was, undeniably, a voice of authority, but Jane couldn't accept what she was hearing. She turned on her aunt angrily. 'You don't understand. Daddy and I . . . Daddy and I were . . .' She floundered. She'd been about to say that she and Gerald had understood one another so well. But she couldn't say that now. How could she, when her father had deceived her—withheld the truth?

'I do understand, Jane. I understand your feelings and I understand your father's. I'd known him many years, bear in mind. I'd known him since long before you were born. You don't see it now, but one day you'll see this as a blessing. The alternative for Gerald would have been very, very painful. And he'd have *hated* being the total burden he would have become. That much, you know as well as I. That much, you must see for yourself.'

'I don't see anything!' Jane shouted. 'I don't see anything except that Daddy died before he should have. I don't see this as a blessing! And *you* don't know what had been going on. You don't know about the shock he was given on the day he died—the shock that brought on his attack!'

No, Margaret acknowledged, she didn't know what had been going on. She'd seen Gerald and Jane only once since Moira died, at a family wedding some twelve months earlier. She knew Jane had been engaged briefly. She had seen the change that had taken place in Jane, the hardness that never used to be there. She knew Gerald was worried about his daughter. But as for their day-to-day lives and recent events, she knew nothing but the little Dr Leonard had told her. He had told her about Jane's hysteria on the night Gerald died—triggered when Adam Francis walked into the room.

'No, dear,' she said quietly, 'I don't know what's been happening, except for what Dr Leonard——'

'He knows nothing, either!' Jane was still shouting. 'He doesn't know the facts.'

'Then tell me about it, Jane. Tell me how he fits into all this, the man who came to talk to you at the flat. Your boy-friend.'

'Boy-friend!' Jane's laughter was raucous, hollow, horrible. 'Adam Francis is nobody's "boy-friend"! And you should never have let him into my room!'

'But he's in love with you, Jane. That much was obvious to me!'

'I hate him!' Jane shrieked. 'He's responsible for Daddy's death. And do you know what he was doing at the time Daddy died? Raping me, that's what he was doing!'

Jane didn't wait for a reaction. She bolted from the room.

Margaret MacKenzie shook her head sadly. She took that bit of information with the pinch of salt it deserved. It was all a muddle, very much so. The doctor had said something about marriage having been on the cards—that Jane had screamed about it to Mr Francis when she was hysterical.

She sighed. If she didn't know what was going on, she was limited as to the help she could give her niece. But she was also limited as to how far she could push her. She had seen the rigidity in Jane's body, the change in her pupils as soon as Adam Francis had been brought into the conversation. And now Jane had fled, on the verge of hysteria again.

Margaret steeled herself to stay put. For the moment, Jane must be alone. With any luck she would fling herself on her bed and sob it all out.

When the front door slammed shut, Margaret's heart sank. Another walk. If only she'd *cry*. Margaret's eyes moved worriedly towards the windows. It was late, pitch dark outside and bitterly cold. As an aunt, she wanted to run after Jane and pull her back into the safety of the house. As a woman with a great deal of common sense, she knew that would do no good at all.

She stayed where she was.

It was true, of course. It was so typical of Gerald, it was inescapably true.

Jane's eyes flitted to the clock on the mantelpiece. It

was turned three. Aunt Margaret was often late getting home from work, but Jane was missing her today. More than a week had passed since her fraught conversation with her aunt. Another week. A week of nothingness, nothing but going round and round in circles until she thought her head would burst.

But so much was clearer now. She could no longer deny the rightness of what her aunt had said, much as she'd tried to. There was still a lot of fog around, a great deal which she would probably never understand, but at least some of it had lifted. Certain things had become crystal clear.

'. . . He was trying to protect you.'

He always had. Not once had he let Jane go to the doctor's with him—or to the hospital. Jane hated hospitals; she had a fear of them. She had felt that way ever since she had been obliged to spend six weeks in one as a child. Even the smell of them turned her stomach. Her father had tried to protect her from all that, from the depressing side of his life. Why, he had never actually admitted to feeling ill at all. Not once.

Jane squeezed her eyes shut, her fingernails digging into her palms. She was sitting in the window seat of the living room. The snow had turned to filthy slush and it was grey outside, a light, steady drizzle falling.

And yes, he had had a fear of becoming a burden. He had clung to his independence, writing his articles, insisting on cooking, doing what he could around the flat—and making Jane go out when she didn't want to leave him. But he shouldn't have withheld the truth from her! She could have coped with the truth. She *could*! If only she'd known, she would never have left him alone.

'That's obviously the reason he didn't tell you.'

Aunt Margaret's words went round and round in her head, refusing to be silenced. Gerald simply hadn't wanted her to know the real extent of his illness. She put trembling fingers to her temples. She had tried not to think about this, she still didn't want to, but she had to accept the real reason for her father's deceit. And the real reason had nothing to do with Jane's loathing of hospitals. Gerald had kept the truth from her because he wanted her to get on with her own life. Hadn't he told her often enough to do precisely that?

And what had she done instead? She had deceived him in return, by pretending she was going out with Paul Meekins.

She groaned, aloud, staring out into the greyness of the day. Deceit was far too strong a word. What they had done to each other had been for the best possible reasons, after all. She laughed hollowly. What strange things people did in the name of love! What extremes they'd gone to in an effort to protect——

The scream shattered Jane's thoughts, brought her quickly to her feet. It was very close but she couldn't tell which direction it came from. It was the high-pitched, frightened scream of a child.

'Jimmy!'

She flew outside, calling his name. There was no answer. Jane stood still, straining to hear a sound, but there was nothing but the silence of the drizzle, the stillness of the quiet lane. She looked up and down the road, over at the nearby fields. Nothing. She skirted the house, walking right round it till she was back at the garden gate. And then she heard a sob. 'Jimmy? Is it you, Jimmy? Where are you?'

Jane opened the gate. He was at the bottom of the back garden, lying in a crumpled heap at the foot of the five-foot wall which kept the wind off the garden in the summertime. She hurried over to him and stopped in her tracks as he recoiled from her, struggling with obvious difficulty into a sitting position. The fringe of his red hair was plastered against his forehead and he was covered with the mud of the soil he had landed on.

'Jimmy, why didn't you answer me? How did you——' She saw his knee, streaming with blood, and the brick sticking up from the soil. 'Oh, Jimmy——'

'Go away!' he shouted. 'I don't want you. I want Margaret.' But his voice was shaky and his bottom lip was trembling as he fought not to cry. 'You hate me! You shut the door on me! Don't come near me!'

Jane closed her eyes. The little boy looked positively afraid of her, and for a moment she didn't know what to do about it. She was appalled, disgusted with herself, thinking of the way she had treated him. Had she been so desensitised that she couldn't cope with the innocent inquisitiveness of a six-year-old? What was happening to her? The fear in Jimmy's eyes shocked her into asking the question.

As for her aunt—what must she think? Jane had never even apologised for the way she had screamed at her. And she had never said a word about the way she had treated her little neighbour, and she must know; Jimmy's mother must have said something.

'Jimmy, I—I'm sorry for shouting at you, and closing the door. Please forgive me. I'm very sorry.'

He shook his head, impatiently wiping a tear from his cheek, too proud to let her see it. Then his filthy, muddy hands closed over the wound on his knee.

Jane cringed inwardly, but she made no move to go nearer to him. 'Jimmy, I've been—very mixed up lately—and I didn't realise what I was saying. Let me help you now, please.'

Jimmy looked very dubious indeed. 'No. I can go home. My mum will make it better.'

'But Margaret's got a big box of bandages in the house—and special ointment that will make your leg better.'

His interest was captured. 'Bandages? Will it need bandages? Is it a nurse's box?'

'Yes.' Jane smiled, fighting against the constriction in her throat. 'A special one—from the hospital.'

It took him two seconds to decide. Two seconds in which he weighed her up and decided she was probably trustworthy, after all. 'Okay. You can do it, then.'

Jane scooped him up and carried him indoors, placing him gently in the big armchair by the fire— Margaret's chair. 'I'm sure Margaret won't mind if you sit in her chair, Jimmy. She isn't home from work yet.'

Jane's eyes moved to the clock and Jimmy's followed. 'I know. I can tell the time, you know. Well—almost. I know it's more than three o'clock, anyway.'

Jane moved swiftly, fetching the first aid box and a bowl of water. She set it down by Jimmy's feet and poured antiseptic into the water.

'Pooh! I don't like the smell of that!' Jimmy protested, picking up the first aid box and looking into it as if it were something fascinating.

'Neither do I,' Jane said truthfully, flinching as she started to clean the wound. It was a nasty cut, embedded with mud, but not in need of a stitch. 'Darling, don't touch anything in there. Wait till I've washed your hands.'

Jimmy looked at her as if she were the lowest thing on earth. 'Darling?' he said disgustedly. 'Don't call me that! It's too soppy! That's what they say to each other on the telly!'

Jane laughed. 'Is it really? Well, I'd better not say it again!' She giggled, marvelling at the way he was so easily distracted from what she was doing to him. She knew his knee must be stinging like fury. He was a hardy little boy, and bright.

He cocked his head to one side. 'It's nice when you

laugh, Jane. You never laughed before. Are you better now?'

She swallowed hard, fighting not to cry. The last thing she wanted was to alarm Jimmy now. She nodded. 'Why—why were you climbing over the garden wall?'

'I wasn't, silly. I—ooh, that stuff's cold!—I was standing on the wall waiting for Margaret. I was going to wave to her when I saw her in the kitchen, then I knew she'd come out and talk to me. But I slipped off 'cos it was wet.'

Jane groaned inwardly with self-loathing, her eyes filling with tears despite her efforts.

'Why hasn't Margaret come home?' He started fiddling with Jane's hair as she bandaged his knee with trembling hands.

'I don't know, dar—Jimmy. There's probably been an emergency.'

'What's an emergency?'

'It's—well, it's like this.' She patted his leg. 'It's when something happens and you weren't expecting it to.'

'Your hair's all wet. It's dangling.' He leaned forward, fiddling with her slide until it opened and her hair cascaded round her shoulders. 'There!' he said with relish. 'That's pretty. You shouldn't tie your hair up, Jane. My big sister doesn't.'

Jane's hands were shaking so much that she had to take off the bandage and start again. It was taking all she had to fight against her tears. 'W—why aren't you in school today? The doctor said you could go back.'

Jimmy wailed, suddenly losing all patience with her. 'It's Sunday. I've *told* you, you don't go to school on Sundays.'

'It's——' She blinked, her eyes misty as she secured the bandage. Sunday. Again. She'd been here over three weeks . . .

'I—I didn't realise I'd been . . . I told you, Jimmy, I've been mixed up lately.'

'Yes, but you should know what day it is! Don't you know the days?'

'I do now. There, you're patched up. We'll just——'

Betsy, who had been sleeping peacefully by the fire, started barking furiously. Jane let out a long, slow, sigh of relief. Her aunt's homecoming was always heralded by the old dog's barking.

Margaret took in the scene with one swift glance, seeing instantly the state of her niece and her nearness to tears. She was smiling, though to Jane she looked incredibly tired.

'So! What's been going on here?' She walked over to Jimmy and ruffled his hair, all the time watching Jane, who was fiddling with the first aid box, keeping her head averted.

There followed a detailed account from Jimmy, who exaggerated everything, including Jane's kindness and efficiency. 'Did you have an emergency?' he added, looking to Jane for approval.

'Yes,' Margaret laughed. 'Come on, laddie, I'll take you home now you're all fixed up.'

'No!' the boy protested loudly. 'Jane and I are friends now. And she's going to wash my hands. And we're talking.'

'Tomorrow,' Margaret said firmly, watching Jane. 'You can come back tomorrow, Jimmy, and talk to Jane then.'

'Can I?' He looked to the younger woman for confirmation. 'If I go home now, can I come back and see you tomorrow, after school?'

Jane nodded, not trusting herself to speak.

'Promise? . . . No, you've got to say it, Jane!'

'Promise,' she whispered.

She exchanged looks with her aunt as Margaret

carried the boy out of the room. Immediately the front door closed, Jane virtually collapsed on the rug as the dam burst and she sobbed her heart out. She cried as she had never cried before; not when she was a child, not when she lost her mother, or her fiancé. Utterly wretched, she sobbed and sobbed, and the tears just kept on coming. Betsy, confused, stood over her whining and nuzzling as if in sympathy with her.

Then she felt the warmth of her aunt's arms around her as she was coaxed, half lifted on to the settee. Margaret held her very tightly as she sobbed, stroking her hair—and saying nothing to encourage her to stop. Her own eyes were full of tears—tears of relief. Jane's feeling of guilt had finally been exorcised, and her sobbing was the best thing Margaret had heard in a long time. She closed her eyes, happy with Jane's progress but unsure how far it went.. Jane was no longer blaming herself for her father's death—but was she still placing the responsibility for it in the lap of Adam Francis?

Jane's weeping went on for a long time, until it was she herself who brought it to an end. She went into a coughing fit, her eyes so swollen she could hardly see out of them. 'I—I'm sorry, Aunt Margaret.'

'Don't be.'

'I—I'm all right now.' Jane got unsteadily to her feet. 'Please—you go and have your rest. I'll bring you a cup of tea.'

'Oh, that's all right, hen.' Margaret always used the Scottish endearment when she was at her most indulgent. 'I'll put the kettle on.'

'No.' Jane's voice was steady now. 'You go and take your nap. Please let me do something for you. Heaven knows, I've done nothing in all this time!'

Margaret got to her feet, smiling. 'Well, remember to give it two for the pot!'

Jane busied herself in the kitchen, making the tea

just as her aunt liked it—so strong she could almost stand the spoon up in it.

She took it upstairs, only to find Margaret fast asleep on her bed. Jane stood at her side, watching her. She always took a nap when she got back from the hospital, but she hadn't even bothered to take off her uniform today, or even her shoes.

Jane undid her aunt's belt, removed her shoes and covered her with a blanket. She went down to the kitchen and made herself some coffee, a fresh bout of tears spilling down her cheeks. Her aunt was shattered. She left the house a little after five in the morning and today it had been almost four before she got home.

Jane looked round the kitchen. The stove needed cleaning, her aunt's breakfast dishes stood, washed, on the draining board, but Jane's own dishes hadn't even been brought into the kitchen. In more than three weeks she hadn't done a thing to help her aunt. Margaret had cooked for her, shopped for her, washed for her, and never said a word about it.

She got busy immediately, cleaning the old cooker until it shone as well as it was ever going to shine. She looked in the fridge, decided on what they would have for dinner, and started peeling potatoes.

Margaret found her cleaning the kitchen floor a couple of hours later. She smiled inwardly, making no attempt to admonish. 'Oh, Jane, that is kind. I've been meaning to get round to that for the past three days!'

Jane leaned on the mop, catching her breath. It was a big, old-fashioned kitchen. 'Feeling better for your sleep?'

'Mm. Oh, you've done the cooker, too. Dear me, look at it! What on earth did you clean it with? I've never seen it actually shining before!'

'Elbow grease.' Jane forced herself to smile as more tears threatened. Now she was weepy because her aunt had made no protest, because her kindness knew no bounds.

As soon as Margaret left for work the following morning, Jane attacked the rest of the house, cleaning anything that needed cleaning and anything that didn't. When Jimmy arrived a little after four, he and Margaret were treated to home-made scones, fresh from the oven.

The next day, before the forecast return of the snow, Jane whitewashed the offending back garden wall—another job her aunt had not had a chance to get round to. It was a crazy time of year to do it, Margaret thought, but it served a purpose. She thanked her niece warmly.

In the dining room that evening, over the meal which she had cooked, Jane announced that she was going home.

She saw her aunt's doubtful look, and reassured her. 'It's all right—I'm ready to go now. I'll leave it till Friday, then we can drive to the station on your day off.'

'It isn't that, Jane.' Margaret paused, hating to think of Jane being alone over Christmas. She knew what it was like to be alone over Christmas. 'It's just that I thought you might like to come to Edinburgh with me. I've got time off and I'll be driving down to Alice's on Christmas Eve. Won't you come with me? Your Aunt Alice would be so pleased——'

'No. But thank you. I want to go home. You see—there are a few things I have to do. I mean, clear up. I have to talk to . . . well, it doesn't matter. I'm ready to go, and that's the main thing.'

Margaret looked up quickly but Jane had averted her eyes. 'Well . . . I'm not going to try and persuade you to stay, dear, if you're set on going home.' She pondered over the wisdom of asking Jane a question, unsure whether Jane was ready to answer yet, but

encouraged by what she'd just heard. 'Jane, are you
. . . is it Adam Francis you want to talk to?'

Jane stared at her, wide-eyed, horrified. 'No, it
isn't. It certainly isn't!'

Margaret's mouth opened, but no words came out.
She was utterly confused.

'I'm sorry, I'm sorry,' Jane said hastily, guiltily. 'I
didn't mean to snap at you, Aunt Margaret.'

'Look, Jane, I really feel you should tell me . . . I
think—well, I feel I have a right to know . . . What
was it Adam Francis said to Gerald on the day he
died?'

Jane didn't hesitate. 'That he intended to marry
me.' It wasn't until she saw her aunt's look of
complete bewilderment that she realised how stupid
that sounded in the light of her accusations about
Adam. But her aunt really didn't understand . . .

Margaret said so. 'I don't understand. You've lost
me. Why—why did you think that would be a shock to
your father? Oh!' Her hand went to her mouth. 'I see,
I see,' she went on, her frown disappearing as she
worked it out for herself. 'Gerald disliked Adam, is
that it? He disapproved of him . . .'

Jane actually squirmed in her seat. 'Well, no . . . he
liked him very much, actually . . .'

There was a long silence.

Jane looked away, feeling utterly stupid in her
aunt's eyes but justifying herself to herself by
remembering that Margaret didn't know all the facts,
not by any means.

Margaret's frown was back—and disappeared again.
'So Adam wanted you to live in his country? He didn't
want Gerald to live with you, is that it? He was
thinking you'd put your father into a nursing home or
something?'

'No. No. Oh, leave me alone, will you? I'm
sorry—I just don't want to talk about Adam. I can't

even bear to think about him!' Jane got to her feet, started clearing the table hastily and headed for the kitchen.

Margaret went into the living room and stoked the fire. She sat down wearily, shaking her head. Jane obviously still had a lot of sorting out to do—with her life and within herself. But at that moment, Margaret's concern was not for her niece. She was thinking about the tall, attractive man who was in love with Jane, she was thinking about the pain she'd seen in his eyes as he had left the flat. Jane had suffered, was still suffering, but Margaret realised that Adam Francis was suffering equally.

She said no more to Jane until they were standing on the railway station on Friday morning.

'Goodbye, Aunt Margaret.' Jane hugged her aunt, unable to thank her enough for her kindness. 'I'm so grateful to you, I can't tell you——'

'Hush, child! That's what families are for. Now you'll write to me, you promise?'

'Of course.'

'And if . . . if you do want to talk . . . I mean, if you do want to talk about Adam, you can always phone me——'

Jane picked up her case. 'I'd better get on board. The train's due out in three minutes.'

'Jane——' Margaret reached for her arm as she turned away.

'I don't want to talk about it,' Jane said quietly. 'Nor will I.'

'Very well.' Margaret opened the train door for her. 'But there's one thing I must say to you, Jane. Just bear in mind that Adam is as guiltless as you are. You know that already, deep down. You didn't know the extent of Gerald's illness—and neither did Adam.'

'Goodbye, Aunt Margaret. And thank you again.' Jane leaned out of the window, waving to her aunt as the train pulled away from the platform. She stayed there until she could no longer see her aunt, until the icy wind started freezing the tears on her cheeks. 'Adam,' she murmured into the wind. 'Oh, Adam, Adam, Adam . . .'

CHAPTER ELEVEN

JANE'S worst days were the ones that followed after she got home. It was then that she really hit rock bottom. She cried solidly for the first three days.

Each evening, she knocked at Mrs Graham's door. She was anxious to talk to her neighbour, but Mrs Graham was away—probably staying with her son and daughter-in-law over the holidays.

She was anxious to talk to Dr Leonard, too, but when she phoned the surgery she was told that the doctor had gone abroad for two weeks and there was a locum standing in for him.

Jane wished she had stayed in Scotland. The two people she had come home to talk to were not available, and her days were horribly lonely. She fell into the habit of switching the television on from the time she got up to the time she went to bed. Not that she paid much attention to it. It was just on. There. Company.

Night time was the worst. She couldn't sleep. She would lie in bed with the radio on, drinking tea and thinking, thinking, thinking. There was nothing and nobody to provide her with a real distraction. It was a sorry state of affairs, she realised, that she had no friends she could call on. Oh, she had acquaintances, people she had worked with, other neighbours. But it was Christmas, a time for families and friends, and there was nobody in London, nobody at all, whom she could call a friend. Nobody into whose home she could invite herself and feel comfortable. She wasn't that close to anyone these days.

Hadn't Adam once told her she lived in a grey, narrow little world? How succinctly he had put it. How right he had been! Jane's world was very narrow indeed, and it was all her own making. She never used to be like she was now. Things, life, used to be so different. *She* used to be so different. What had happened to her? What had happened to the fun-loving, easygoing girl who used to laugh so readily, who used to be adventurous, lively, generous of self? How could she have changed so radically over the past three years? She had lost touch with the people who used to be her friends. She had lost touch with life, with *herself*.

New Year's Eve found her sitting in front of the television. She watched the Scots having fun in their annual, inevitable, New Year's Eve show.

As a Scot, her mother had always attached a great deal of importance to New Year. She used to say it was a time for review as well as a time for celebration. A time for review. Jane had already started her review, but she had by no means found herself again.

On the morning of New Year's Day, she took a long hard look at herself in her bedroom mirror, and what she saw filled her with disgust. Her physical appearance was appalling. Her hair was lank, unwashed, there were dark circles under her eyes and her face was paler than ever. She was thinner, too. Since she had left Scotland, she hadn't eaten a square meal. She'd been living on snacks.

She wept again. She was not feeling sorry for herself, rather she was filled with self-disgust. She wept for the wretched, useless, person she had become over the past three years. After being jilted by Billy she had locked up her heart, sealed herself off from people, from life.

Adam was right. More and more she was remembering the things he had said to her. He had told her she had been afraid to love. But it was even worse than that—she had been afraid to live, because life hurt sometimes and she had determined that nothing would ever hurt her again. Three years ago she had built the protective barriers around herself, and the saddest thing of all was that now those barriers had been stripped away, it was too late.

Adam wasn't guilty of anything. She had known that all along, deep inside, just as Aunt Margaret had pointed out. What was Adam guilty of—loving her? And what had she given him in return?

He didn't phone her. Despite everything, in a tiny corner of her mind she had dared to hope that he might just ring to ask after her. But of course he wouldn't. She had destroyed any feeling he had for her.

At the end of the week, Mrs Graham came home. Jane heard her front door close and she dashed out immediately, still anxious to talk to her. Mrs Graham had been the last person to speak to her father, and it was for that reason that Jane wanted to see her.

But it wasn't Mrs Graham who had gone into the flat next door, it was her son Robin. 'Oh!' The disappointment on Jane's face was obvious as Robin opened the door to her. 'I'm sorry, I—I thought——'

'Hello. How are you, Jane?'

She smiled at the concern on his face. Jane had only met Robin a couple of times before, briefly. He was a nice enough man, in an ordinary, down-to-earth sort of way. 'I'm all right, thank you.'

'I'm sorry about—about your——'

'Thank you.' She straightened her shoulders. 'I thought it was your mother coming home, actually. Is she here?'

'No, she—I'm so sorry, won't you come in?' He stepped aside, but Jane shook her head. 'Well, she's got the 'flu, I'm afraid.'

'I'm sorry to hear that . . .'

'It's all our fault. First I had it, then the kids had it over Christmas, now Mum's got it. So the least we can do is keep her with us and look after her! I just came to collect some more of her things.' He waved a list at her. 'She didn't trust me to remember everything, so she wrote it down.'

'I see.' Jane tried to keep her voice light as she asked how long Mrs Graham was likely to be away.

'I don't know,' Robin shrugged. 'A week or two, I suppose. Do you want me to give her a message? Is anything wrong? I mean, what I mean is——' He shifted awkwardly, embarrassed by his own question.

'No, no,' Jane said hastily. 'I just wanted to wish her a happy New Year, that's all.'

Robin looked at her doubtfully. 'Look, Jane, why don't you drive back to Kent with me? You can see Mum, stay with us for the weekend. Angie will be glad to meet you, and you're more than welcome——'

Jane was shaking her head, but she thanked him profusely, touched by his gesture. 'It's very kind of you, Robin, and I appreciate it. But really, I'm fine— honestly. Just give my love to your mum, wish her happy New Year.'

'If you're sure . . .'

Jane went back into her own flat, trembling with disappointment. What she wanted to ask Mrs Graham had to be asked in private. Had Gerald said anything to her about Jane getting married? That was what she wanted to know. Something, at least, must have been said at some point, because Mrs Graham had used Adam's name when Jane was screaming at him. That recollection had come to Jane in Scotland, when her mental fog had finally started to lift. So Gerald must have described Adam to Mrs Graham in some manner. In what manner? In what context?

She went into the kitchen and put the kettle on for

coffee. But what did it matter, really? Whatever had been said, what difference did it make? What kind of fool was she to think there might still be hope for her and Adam?

She loved him, and he had loved her. But she had thrown Adam's love back in his face. All along the line she had insulted him or lied to him, mistrusted, doubted, until finally she had accused him of——

That didn't bear thinking about.

She had destroyed Adam's love for her, and it had to be faced: she'd lost him for ever.

Feeling as if her legs were about to give way beneath her, Jane leaned heavily against the kitchen wall, holding on to the sink for support. Coming back to life again, facing things, was a difficult and very painful process. But reality was being forced upon her and she had, finally, to face herself, her mistakes.

Turning towards the kitchen window, she looked up at an insipid sun shining from a cold, clear sky. She looked down at the cars parked in the courtyard, her own, long neglected Mini among them. It was time to go out and face the world, too. Time to put her life into some semblance of order.

During the next couple of weeks Jane almost managed to do just that. She spent some of the savings she no longer needed and traded her car in for a much newer model. She would use it to travel to work in; she decided to work locally since she no longer needed to work for the maximum amount of money. There was plenty of temporary work in West London for a secretary with her qualifications. Her days in the City, in offices like those of David Boyd or Brinkman, Clayton & Brinkman, were a thing of the past. She wanted to temp because she wanted to put some variation into her work.

With the demands of constantly changing offices,

and work of an unfamiliar nature, she might, she just might, be able to distract her mind from thoughts of Adam. During the day, at least. She signed on at a local agency and by the time Mrs Graham came home, she had already completed her first week's work.

It was the beginning of February. Jane was having a lie-in when she heard Mrs Graham's door closing on the Saturday morning. But she made no move to get out of bed. Not immediately, anyway. She didn't need to. She no longer needed to ask Mrs Graham what, if anything, Gerald had said. She knew what he had said to Adam, and that was all that mattered. She knew exactly what he had said to Adam, because Adam had told her. She knew also that Gerald had died a happy man, because Adam had told her that, too.

Being back at work hadn't stopped Jane from thinking about the man she had loved and lost. Managing to sleep most nights didn't keep him out of her mind, either. Adam Francis was in her dreams, in her blood and in her every waking moment more strongly than ever, because she loved him more than ever.

There were so many things she understood now. About herself, about her father, the things Adam had tried to point out to her on the evening he proposed. Her recollection of that night had become complete.

If only she'd known herself before! If only she had given Adam the love and respect he deserved, responded to him as a woman instead of as a frightened girl—the mixed-up kid he had so rightly accused her of being.

She remembered the last thing he had said to her, too. The very last thing: that he would be waiting, that when she came through the trauma he would be waiting for her.

If only she could believe that!

She got out of bed and took a quick shower. She was in no hurry to see Mrs Graham, but Mrs Graham would obviously want to see her. She put some make-up on, slipped into a pair of denims and a sweater, and no sooner had she finished dressing than Mrs Graham came round.

'Jane, my dear, you look quite well! Robin said—I mean . . .'

'I can imagine what Robin told you, but I'm much better now. I've started eating since then—properly! Come in, Mrs Graham, I'll make some tea.' She saw the elderly lady's eyes flit quickly around the living room, and she swallowed against the lump in her throat, knowing what Mrs Graham was thinking, feeling. She went hastily into the kitchen and busied herself with the tea tray.

She would have to sell this flat. She had known that for some time now, but she had not yet done anything about it. There were too many memories here, of Gerald, of the ruggedly attractive man who had sat here and talked and laughed with him. It wasn't healthy to be constantly reminded of all she had lost. If she were to give herself a proper chance at starting a new life, she would have to sell the flat.

'You've had your hair permed. It looks very nice.' Jane poured out the tea and handed a cup to her neighbour.

'Do you think so? My daughter-in-law talked me into it. She said it would give me a lift.'

'And has it? Are you better now?'

Mrs Graham looked heavenward. 'Coming home has given me a lift. Oh, don't misunderstand me, dear—it was nice to be with my family, but it's very nice to come home. I've missed my little part-time job, and frankly the children were getting to be a bit much. The boy's six and the girl's five, and Robin doesn't discipline them as he should.' She paused, considering. 'Unless it's me—getting less tolerant in my old age.'

'Now, now,' Jane laughed. 'Less of the old age

business! I happen to know you're only a year older than Daddy was.' She saw Mrs Graham's quick, uncertain look, and added, 'It's all right, I can talk about it now.'

'Jane . . .' The older woman fidgeted uncomfortably. 'You seem well enough, but how—how is everything, really?'

'I'm all right.' Jane's response was quick. The worst was over, and she knew she looked acceptable, almost back to normal. And the pain that was her love for Adam didn't show. It was constantly there, in her heart, but with the aid of make-up and a bright smile, it was not reflected in her face. 'I've bought myself a new car, and I've been working for a week now.'

She saw Mrs Graham's frown, and braced herself.

'Working? But I thought . . . I mean, it's been almost three months since the funeral and I was wondering if you were still—if you'd set your wedding date?'

Jane put down her cup. 'So Daddy did mention that to you. He told you about Adam Francis.'

'Mention it? Jane, he talked about it for two hours! He came in here as soon as Mr Francis left him that day. And of course I knew it was Mr Francis you'd stayed with in the Caribbean, when you got stranded because of a strike or something.'

'Really?' Jane looked at her quickly. She hadn't realised before quite how friendly Gerald had been with their neighbour. 'You and Daddy talked quite a lot, didn't you?'

'Almost every afternoon,' Mrs Graham said proudly. 'But I never saw him as happy as he was when Mr Francis had been here and said you were getting married.'

'I know about that,' Jane said hastily. 'Adam told me Daddy's reaction.' She refilled her cup with hands that had started to tremble. This was getting to be a

little more than she could stand. Thinking about
Adam was painful enough, without actually talking
about him.

Mrs Graham gave a satisfied nod. 'Of course he did.
Oh, I'm so glad you two got it sorted out. You said
some . . . well, you were distraught that night, and
your young man obviously understood that. So when
is your big day?'

Jane's eyes closed involuntarily. 'Mrs Graham,
you've got it . . . you've got it all wrong. Things are
not how they seem. I mean, Adam and I are not
getting married.' She looked directly at her neighbour,
then immediately averted her eyes. Mrs Graham's
curious gaze was more than she could bear. 'You see, I
was never really sure. I mean, I'd known Adam such a
short time, and . . .' Her voice faded away.

There was a long, awkward silence. Neither of them
knew what to say next.

Mrs Graham was inspired first. 'Well,' she said, in a
voice whose reasonableness did nothing to hide her
confusion, 'I suppose it was a very short courtship.'

The old-fashioned word made Jane smile inwardly.
What she and Adam had been through could hardly be
described as courting! But Mrs Graham was being
tactful, and it was sweet of her. 'Yes,' she said softly,
'a very short courtship.'

Mrs Graham got to her feet, saying something about
not having unpacked her suitcase yet, and Jane felt a
sudden rush of sympathy. She stood up quickly and
gave her a quick hug. 'Thank you for coming to see
me.'

Mrs Graham smiled, then shrugged a little
helplessly. 'I'm sorry, Jane, I should just mind my
own business. But don't be a stranger to me, dear. Pop
in and see me any time you like.'

Life went on. Jane busied herself as much as she
could. She had three different assignments over the

next five weeks, and it was the second week of March when Dr Leonard came to see her.

Several times she had been asked out, but she had replied with her stock answer. 'Sorry, I'm afraid I can't have dinner with you ... Mm? ... Oh, I thought I'd mentioned ... Yes, deeply involved.'

But it wasn't history repeating itself. She used her stock answer now because it was simply the truth. She was deeply involved—more than that—with Adam Francis. And there would never be anyone else for her.

There was order in her life now, but without Adam there was still no meaning in it. She did go out occasionally, alone. She made herself do it. She made herself function so that nobody guessed there was a broken heart behind the calm façade and the beautiful face.

Nobody except Dr Leonard.

Jane was washing up when he called. There were some people coming to view the flat at eight o'clock, but it was only a quarter past seven. She looked at her watch when the doorbell rang, thinking her prospective buyers had got their wires crossed somewhere along the line.

'Doctor Leonard!' She was surprised and pleased to see him. 'Come in, come in. How are you?'

'I might ask you the same question.' His tone was mild, as was his West Country accent, but Jane looked at him uncertainly as he sat down.

Dr Leonard was in his mid-fifties, a little overweight, but still quite a handsome man. He seemed very slightly irritated.

'Will you have a drink, Doctor? Sherry? Coffee?'

'Give me a small gin, would you, Jane? And fill it up with tonic.'

Jane mixed his drink, poured herself a sherry and sat down facing him. 'What's the matter?'

'I asked you to come and see me when you got back from Scotland. Don't you remember?'

'Yes, I remember,' Jane said pleasantly. Then, a little stiffly, she added, 'I remember everything. And I owe you an apology, I know.'

The doctor dismissed that with a wave of his arm. 'So how long have you been back? And why haven't you been to see me?'

'Well, I came back before Christmas, and I phoned the surgery——'

'Before Christmas?' His surprise was evident, and Jane felt quite pleased with herself.

'Yes. And you can see for yourself that I'm well— and coping. I'm back at work, too.'

Dr Leonard was quiet for a moment, his scrutiny taking in the details of her face before it shifted to his surroundings. He smiled, seeming satisfied. 'The flat's looking nice—spotless. You've been keeping busy, then?'

'Very.' Jane thought it an innocent question and she answered it accordingly.

'Have you kept in touch with your aunt?'

'I've written to her every week.'

Dr Leonard sat back in his chair, making himself quite comfortable. 'You were saying, you phoned the surgery. I took my wife away over Christmas. But you didn't make an appointment with my locum.'

'Of course not. I wasn't ill, Doctor. And even if I were, I'd be loath to see anyone else. After all, you brought me into this world.'

'That's right. And I know your history.' The doctor smiled, but his words made Jane uneasy. This was no social visit, she realised suddenly.

She opened up to him slightly. It wasn't a difficult thing to do with Dr Leonard, and she wanted to let him know of her progress. 'I didn't make an appointment in the New Year, because what I'd wanted to ask you, I'd worked out for myself.' She shrugged. 'I was going to ask why you personally hadn't told me about Daddy's complication. I was angry about that—very. But apart from the fact that you never saw me, you couldn't have told me even if you'd wanted to ... Professional confidentiality, and all that.'

Dr Leonard said nothing. He just raised his bushy eyebrows slightly and looked at her expectantly.

Jane smiled at him. 'You couldn't act against your patient's express wishes.' She spoke slowly, letting him know just how much she'd worked out. 'And Daddy didn't want me to know. It's as simple as that. All he wanted was for me to get on with my life.'

Their eyes met in understanding and she nodded slowly. 'Daddy must have talked to you about me— quite a bit. I worried about him, obviously. But I've only just started to realise how much he worried about me.' She laughed slightly, but it was defensive laughter. 'A fine pair, weren't we?'

'Weren't you.' Dr Leonard smiled warmly, his kind eyes not leaving hers for a second. 'But let's keep a balance on things. Don't be too hard on yourself. After all, in a very short space of time you lost your mother, your fiancé, and it was my unpleasant task to tell you of your father's prognosis. You lost faith—in life, in people. Your father understood all that. He said you'd never recover until you started trusting again. So, when he found out about his heart, he said he'd make certain you didn't. I challenged him over it; he could have spared you some of the shock you've been through, but he was adamant—a stubborn devil, as you know.'

He smiled, took a sip of his drink, and looked at her levelly. 'And he came back at me with something totally unarguable. I quote: "If my heart packs up, there'll not be a darn thing anyone can do about it.

Including you, John. So shut up." He was right, of course. And what happened could have happened at any time.'

Jane heard what he'd said, every single word, but one sentence was going round and round in her head ... He said you'd never recover until you started trusting again ... 'I know. I no longer feel guilty, if that's what you're worried about.'

She wished he'd go. She wanted to think. And there were people coming in ten minutes ...

'I'm glad to hear it. And what about Mr Francis?'

Jane stiffened. She got to her feet. 'Mr Francis isn't guilty, either. Obviously.'

'You've seen him?'

'No ... no. I—er—you must excuse me now, Doctor. I've got some people coming to view the flat shortly.' She looked away, agitated, and suddenly very, very disturbed. 'I—I'm selling the flat.'

Dr Leonard grunted. 'I saw the estate agents' board outside when I happened to visit someone else in the building. That's how I knew you were home. I guessed it would be your flat.' He stood up, and his next words came so casually that it was a moment before they registered with Jane. 'So where are you running to?'

Jane looked at him quickly, her face blanching visibly. 'Running? What do you mean—running?'

'Did I say that?' The doctor's heavy eyebrows twitched slightly. 'It must have been a slip of the tongue. I meant to say going. Where are you going to?'

'I—I ...' She was so disturbed, she could hardly answer him. 'I don't know yet. I'll stay in the area, but I just want to get away from this flat.' She squared her shoulders, meeting his steady gaze. 'I'm getting on with my life, finally.'

The doctor's face was impassive. 'Of course you are.'

The doorbell rang, and Jane dithered where she stood. 'Drat! They're early, and I haven't finished washing the pots yet! Look,' she blurted, 'I want to make it quite clear to you that I'm not running anywhere.'

'Of course you're not. Er—shouldn't you answer the door?'

Dr Leonard followed her, excused himself to the visitors, gave Jane an enigmatic smile, and left.

Jane, utterly confused, twittered stupidly to the couple standing at her front door. 'I'm sorry—do come in. You're early. I mean ... Oh, not that it matters! Er—this is the living room. I haven't finished washing the pots yet.'

She couldn't concentrate. She walked round the flat like something resembling a robot and neglected to mention half of the good points she'd made a mental list of.

As soon as the couple left, Jane poured herself a stiff drink and sank wearily into an armchair.

Running?

Was that what she was doing?

No, no, she was trying to make a fresh start, that was all. Running from what, anyway? From memories? *From Adam?* He'd told her often enough that she couldn't run away from him. 'Dear heaven,' she whispered, 'I'm not trying to! I don't want to!' Everything in her was crying out for him. She wanted to run to him, not away from him.

If only she could! She'd thought of little but Adam for so long. It had been nearly four months since she had seen him, and though he had said he would be waiting for her, he had never attempted to make contact with her.

Adam wasn't waiting for anyone ... unless, unless ... Maybe it was up to her? Maybe he had meant his last words literally, and she had to go to him? No.

Besides, she couldn't do that. She couldn't possibly go to him. She couldn't bear his rejection. Even if he still loved her a little, it wouldn't be enough for her. Not by any means.

She got up, took a hot bath and went to bed early, knowing it was pointless even as she did so. She had a hard week at work and her body was tired. But her mind was racing uncontrollably, with thoughts tumbling round her head like beads in a kaleidoscope, though there was no pattern to them.

Her pillow had never been so uncomfortable. The light was off, it was quiet outside, but sleep was impossible. Adam had loved her once, of that she was certain, but what now? What would he be like now? Perhaps she had transferred all her own problems, past problems, to him. She had treated him so badly and hurt him terribly. He might have sealed off his heart, as she had once done. Against her. Against any woman ... but especially against her. What a waste, what a dreadful, dreadful waste of love that would be. Love. Adam said it was the most precious thing in the world ...

Eventually Jane slept—lightly, fitfully, and not for long. Dreams tormented her, the jumble of her thoughts still chasing each other in her sleep. Or half sleep. Perhaps she wasn't sleeping at all, the voices in her head were so clear, so loud.

... You feared you wouldn't be loved enough. *Enough*, Jane ...

... You don't trust me fully ...

... I love you enough to take on the whole world ...

Jane's eyes flew open, she sat bolt upright, and a single word spilled from her lips. 'Trust.'

She flung the covers from her bed and stumbled across the room, groping for her jeans in the wardrobe. Adam was waiting for her, and she had to get to him as quickly as she possibly could.

CHAPTER TWELVE

EVERYTHING made sense now. Everything in the whole world made sense. In Jane's mind there was calmness, order, clarity, sanity.

She drove as quickly as she dared. The roads were almost deserted, the streets empty. The night was still and from a clear, black sky, a full moon was shining. It was two o'clock in the morning.

Adam was waiting for her. He'd been waiting all along. 'With patience, understanding and demonstration,' he had said, 'I'll prove to you that I love you completely.' A single tear trickled from the corner of Jane's eyes. He shouldn't have needed to demonstrate his love in this way, but she had left left him with no alternative. He shouldn't have been made to suffer, but he had.

For several minutes she drove round in circles, searching for the mews where Adam had driven her, though she had no trouble in recognising the house he had rented. She leapt out of her car and was immediately consumed by suffocating panic. There was no other car there. Hers was the only vehicle on this side of the street.

What if he wasn't in?

For seconds she couldn't think what day it was, but by then she was already slamming the brass door knocker on its hinges. It was Friday, Friday . . . What if he'd gone away for the week-end . . .?

Nothing stirred. The house was in total darkness, but she kept on hammering frantically, desperately.

Dear heavens, it had been four months ... What if he'd gone back to New York? What if ...

The door swung open, and Jane's arms dropped to her sides. She stepped back involuntarily, dazzled by the sudden spillage of light, jumping as a deep, angry voice growled at her. 'What the devil——?'

Time was suspended.

Adam stared at her. He just stared. And Jane stared at him. For how long, she couldn't say, he didn't know. It was as if they were one entity, separate but sharing the same mind, the shock, disbelief, the same overwhelming, overpowering joy.

'Jane . . .' His stare became a gaze and his voice was a caress.

He was barefoot, clad in a pair of old denims and a shirt which was half on and half off. His dark gold mane was shoved back wildly, as if he had raked it with his fingers. Etched into his face there was an unfamiliar tension, the mark of what he had been through. He needed a shave, and his clear, green eyes were still shadowed by sleep.

He was the most beautiful sight in the world.

'Adam ... Oh, Adam, Adam——' Jane moved slowly towards him, her heart pounding frantically as he took her in his arms and held her tightly, tightly, crushing the breath from her.

'Jane! My darling, darling Jane—I thought you'd never come! No—no, that's not true. I knew you'd come to me. You *had* to. But the waiting, the waiting . . .'

Adam closed his eyes and kept perfectly still, just holding Jane in his arms, feeling his heartbeat mingling with hers. This was not a time for words. He wanted to savour this moment. He would never, ever, forget how she looked when he opened the door to find her standing there. His beloved Jane, with the silver moonlight behind her, her long dark hair tumbling round her shoulders, her face reflecting all shc'd suffered and her eyes, those beautiful, almond-shaped eyes, brilliant with love.

He laughed softly, joyously. He laughed until Jane was laughing with him, and crying at the same time. He held her away from him, looking her over, hungry for the sight of her, all of her. Then his laughter exploded, ringing out into the stillness of the night. 'Your socks! And your sweater's inside out! Oh, Jane, look at you!'

'What?' She looked down at her sandal-clad feet, at the blue sock on her right foot and the white one on her left, and their combined laughter echoed round the empty street.

In a house across the way, a bedroom window was flung open and an irate voice yelled at them, 'Have you two quite finished down there?'

Adam scooped Jane up into his arms. 'Not yet!' he yelled back. 'Not yet, my friend!' He carried her over the threshold and kicked the door shut, looking into her eyes as he murmured, 'We're only just starting.' Then his lips came down on hers in a long, exquisitely tender kiss which said more than any words could convey.

He carried her into the moonlit lounge and set her down gently, lowering her from his arms as if she were made of glass, fragile, precious.

Jane smiled up at him, seeing him through a mist of tears. 'I think you'd better close the curtains, darling. We've attracted enough attention as it is!'

He let go of her, reluctantly, and drew the curtains at both ends of the room. Jane switched on a couple of lamps, moved quickly toward the couch as Adam sat, his arms reaching out for her. He kissed her. Again and again he kissed her, his lips brushing away the tears from her cheeks, moving his mouth lightly over her mouth, tasting, savouring its sweetness until Jane could hear nothing but the thudding of her heart.

'No more tears,' he whispered. 'No more, my love. Not ever.'

She reached for his hands, trembling as they lost contact with her body. 'Darling Adam, let me look at you. I just want to look at you.' She drank in the sight of him, searching the strong, familiar features of his face, hungry for the love she saw in the beautiful eyes. His love for her. It had never faltered for a moment.

'That's right,' he said softly. 'I fell in love with you on sight, when I looked into your eyes, your soul.'

'And from that moment on, I was yours.' She was whispering, unable to speak properly. 'I love you, Adam. I love you more than I dreamed it was possible to love. But then I'm only just learning what love is all about.'

Adam tilted her chin up, his scrutiny as concerned, as caring as her own. 'How are you, darling?'

Jane's eyes closed briefly. 'I am strong. I am whole. I was swathed in prejudice and ignorance, and despite how much I'd learnt over these months, it was only just a few hours ago that I came, finally, to understand. Adam ... how can you forgive me so easily, without a question, without a word?'

'For what?' he asked softly. 'For turning into the woman who loves me completely? The woman who trusts me—with her heart, with the rest of her life. Darling, I should be asking forgiveness. My timing was lousy—lousy, Jane. I rushed you. I pushed you so hard that night, expecting too much, too quickly, and you went home to—to——'

Jane put a finger over his lips. 'To seek my father's

approval. Unnecessarily. It was just another symptom, Adam. Of my fears, of my guilt at reaching out for happiness, of my stupidity. I . . . I've been so slow to inherit that which . . .' She broke off. It wasn't difficult to speak. Nothing was difficult now. But she was searching for the right words.

She walked over to the bar and helped herself to a drink, pouring a Scotch for Adam. 'I'm nearly twenty-four years old, and until now I've lacked . . . everything . . . my mother's optimism, my aunt's strength, my father's wisdom. I had none of your perception, your capacity for—Oh, Adam, I've been such a fool! Such a fool!'

'Hey, hey, take it easy! You're talking about my future wife!' Adam's smile was indulgent, and brief. She needed this—to talk, to assess, to absorb. 'Go on, darling. And now?'

Jane sighed. 'Now, I—Well, I hope I have a little of each of those things. I think I have. I've faced myself . . . I know I never fooled Daddy for a moment.' She laughed then, at herself. 'But you know that already. I never fooled you, either. I just fooled myself.'

She moved restlessly round the room, sipping her drink. 'Oh, Daddy believed I was going out with Paul Meekins, just as Paul believed I was going out with David Boyd—but what a mess! What a stupid, stupid mess I was in, and created. I'm only thankful that Daddy never discovered the real extent of it . . .

'When he died, at first I was angry. No, that's not so. At first, I was numb. Then when the numbness wore off I was angry. There was so much anger inside me, I couldn't think straight. And then there came a time when I couldn't do anything but think straight . . .'

She talked and talked, and Adam listened carefully, proud of her, loving her, crazy for her.

'Oh, Adam ... Darling, your timing wasn't bad. You'll never know how grateful I am that you pushed me. You made me understand myself. You made my father happy. He'd wanted so much for me to ... If you hadn't pushed me, if you hadn't loved me so much, you—Dr Leonard must have told you about his heart?'

'Yes.' Adam nodded gravely. 'And you didn't know anything about it, either.'

'He forbade Doctor Leonard to tell me. He— Doctor Leonard came to see me tonight. In fact, if he hadn't come to see me, I might have kept you waiting longer. It might have been a few more weeks before I saw sense, before everything fell into place. But I realised ... that you were waiting. That I had to come to you, just as you'd told me. It was my turn, Adam. My turn to prove that I loved you and trusted you completely.'

'It had to be that way, Jane. Heaven knows I wanted to be with you. The number of times I fought with myself, picked up the phone and put it down again. But I had to. I didn't want you to go through hell all alone. But I couldn't risk——'

'It's all right, darling. I understand. And you were absolutely right. I had to grow up—finally.' Jane sank into a chair, hardly able to keep her eyes open, but still talking, talking. She was exhausted by the emotions of the night, by the wretchedness of the months behind her. But that was where they were, behind her.

She looked at Adam, her eyes feasting on the sight of him. He was tired, though the strain had already left his face. She laughed softly. 'You need a shave! And I'm going to make you a nice cup of tea.'

'Tea? Spare me!' He grinned, pulling her to her feet. 'You can make us some coffee. And make it strong, Jane, very strong. Because if you think you're going to fall asleep on me now, you've got another think coming!' He nuzzled against her ear, his lips trailing sensuously along her throat as his hands moved beneath her sweater. She held him tightly, yielding to the sheer pleasure of his kiss, a kiss that left her trembling with yearning.

Adam groaned softly, his voice thick with desire. 'Hey, what happened to the old Jane? My proper, English ... Now she doesn't even put on her undies when she comes to see me ...'

She giggled, blushing, arching towards him as his hands caressed the softness of her naked breasts.

'It's going to be a beautiful, beautiful honeymoon.' Adam's lips brushed over her face, her eyes. 'Where will it be, my darling? Anywhere in the world. Just name it and we'll take the first flight out of here.' He smiled, that slow, audacious smile which sent shivers through her body. 'But I warn you now, it'll make little difference where we go, because I'm going to keep you indoors for a long, long time.'

'San Pablo,' she murmured. 'San Pablo, of course ... Oh, darling, look! Look. It's morning!'

Through a chink in the curtains there was a shaft of daylight. Adam moaned softly, laughing at her as she wriggled out of his arms. She was still driving him crazy ...

Jane pulled back the curtains and they were bathed in the brilliant glow of the early morning sun, shining into the room from a blue and cloudless sky.

At the back of the house there was a small garden, and a young, solitary tree, tinged with the first hint of green which heralded the spring.

'A new season ... A new day.' She moved into the warm circle of Adam's arms, a smiling, happy, woman. A woman reborn. A woman who was strong, now, in her own right.

She reached out to the man for whom destiny had intended her, the softness of her mouth opening against his lips, and her new life . . . their new life . . . began with that new day.

THE MAN WITH THE GOLDEN TOUCH

Many of the myths and legends of ancient Greece are stories with morals. Some are rather light and humorous, particularly the Dionysiac legends, which are tales revolving around Dionysus, the god of wine. The most famous of these is the story of King Midas, a ruler of ancient Phrygia.

One day, King Midas caught a satyr in his garden; this particular satyr was one of Dionysus's protectors. Midas was a good-natured king and treated his captive well. When Dionysus came to collect the errant satyr he rewarded Midas with a wish. Without thinking of the dreadful consequences, Midas wished that all he touched might turn to gold. How thrilled he was as he passed through his palace, turning his furniture and statues into gold—and quickly becoming extremely wealthy!

His problems began, however, when he sat down to eat, because the food he picked up turned to gold as soon as it touched his mouth. Poor King Midas almost starved to death! Dionysus, laughing merrily at Midas's foolishness, granted him release if he bathed in a certain river—and to this day that river is known to contain traces of gold in its water.

Perhaps this old story is meant to serve as a warning about the oft-dire consequences of greed. But today, when someone is said to have the "Midas touch," as Adam Francis is in *Never Say Never*, it usually means that he is an excellent businessman, for whom all ventures turn out financially successful!

Get this book FREE!

Twice in a Lifetime
REBECCA FLANDERS
Harlequin American Romance

Mail to:

Harlequin Reader Service

In the U.S.
2504 West Southern Avenue
Tempe, AZ 85282

In Canada
649 Ontario Street
Stratford, Ontario N5A 6W2

YES! I want to be one of the first to discover **Harlequin American Romance.** Send me FREE and without obligation *Twice in a Lifetime.* If you do not hear from me after I have examined my FREE book, please send me the 4 new **Harlequin American Romances** each month as soon as they come off the presses. I understand that I will be billed only $2.25 for each book (total $9.00). There are no shipping or handling charges. There is no minimum number of books that I have to purchase. In fact, I may cancel this arrangement at any time. *Twice in a Lifetime* is mine to keep as a FREE gift, even if I do not buy any additional books.

Name _____ (please print) _____

Address _____ Apt. no. _____

City _____ State/Prov. _____ Zip/Postal Code _____

Signature (If under 18, parent or guardian must sign.) _____

Discover the new and unique

Harlequin Category-Romance Specials!

Regency Romance
A DEBT OF HONOR
Mollie Ashton

THE FAIRFAX BREW
Sara Orwig

Gothic Romance
THE SATYR RING
Alison Quinn

THE RAVENS
OF ROCKHURST
Marian Martin

Romantic Suspense
THE SEVENTH GATE
Dolores Holliday

THE GOBLIN TREE
Robyn Anzelon

A new and exciting world of romance reading

Harlequin Category-Romance Specials